# FIREWORKS

★　　★　　★　　★　　★　　★　　★

MISTLETOE: FOUR HOLIDAY STORIES

By Hailey Abbott, Melissa de la Cruz,
Aimee Friedman, Nina Malkin


POOL BOYS

By Erin Haft


SUMMER BOYS
NEXT SUMMER: A SUMMER BOYS NOVEL
AFTER SUMMER: A SUMMER BOYS NOVEL
LAST SUMMER: A SUMMER BOYS NOVEL

By Hailey Abbott


SOUTH BEACH
FRENCH KISS
HOLLYWOOD HILLS

By Aimee Friedman

# FIREWORKS

★ ★ ★ ★ ★ ★ ★

FOUR SUMMER STORIES BY

Niki Burnham

Erin Haft

Sarah Mlynowski

Lauren Myracle

SCHOLASTIC INC.

NEW YORK ★ TORONTO ★ LONDON ★ AUCKLAND ★ SYDNEY
MEXICO CITY ★ NEW DELHI ★ HONG KONG ★ BUENOS AIRES

No part of this work may be reproduced, stored in a retrieval system, or transmitted in any form or by any means, electronic, mechanical, photocopying, recording, or otherwise, without written permission of the publisher. For information regarding permission, write to Scholastic Inc., Attention: Permissions Department, 557 Broadway, New York, NY 10012.

ISBN-13: 978-0-439-90300-4
ISBN-10: 0-439-90300-9

12  11  10  9  8  7  6  5  4  3  2  1     7  8  9  10  11  12/0

Printed in the U.S.A.
First printing, April 2007

★ ★ ★ ★ ★ ★ ★

# MISS
# INDEPENDENT

By Lauren Myracle

★ ★ ★ ★ ★ ★ ★

The sun is delicious on my skin as I drift lazily in my cousin Porter Ann's pool. Lazy is the only word for it, lazy and warm and yet not *too* warm, since cool water sluices onto my float when I dip my leg over the side. Or when Porter Ann flicks droplets on me, like right now.

"Quit it," I say, but I don't mean it. If I meant it, I wouldn't say it. Porter Ann is one year older than me and "wild" (that's the word my parents use), and if she thought I honestly didn't want her splashing me, she'd do it even more.

Plus, the water feels good. My skin feels good. I feel liquid and soft, like caramel, and my insides expand with hopefulness. And why not? *Today is my birthday*, I tell myself. *Today I'm eighteen. And why shouldn't something wonderful happen? It could! It's possible!*

I'm ready for something wonderful, that's for sure. I feel as if I've lived my whole life just waiting. And watching. And then — tragically — running and hiding when anything potentially wonder-filled comes my way.

I think of Pete, and I sigh. Pete was wonderful, there's no denying it. And yet — case in point — I was an absolute and total wimp the one chance I had to do something about it. To reach out and connect with another human being, what could be more important than that? And not even in a physical way, although that would be nice, too. But what I want, what I wish for with all my heart, is to connect with someone in a way that goes beyond flirting and posturing and trying to impress.

When Pete's eyes met mine that one time, on the last day he was helping his dad do repairs at the preschool building, I felt something pass between us. I'd been noticing him all week, and I'm fairly sure he'd noticed me, too. I had that special, tingly, ultra-awareness whenever I was around him, and it seems to me that when one person feels that way, usually the other person does, too. Or maybe that's just me being a dreamer?

Porter Ann's a pragmatist, and she claims that what someone feels doesn't matter. It's what a person *does* that makes a difference. And since I was a big baby and did nothing, I forfeited the right to moan and sigh and long for Pete — especially since it's unlikely I'll ever see him again.

"You never even kissed the guy!" she exclaimed when I tried to tell her how I felt. "Forget that — you never exchanged more than three words with him!"

"Six," I said. "Six words." I wasn't giving up what little I had.

She threw up her hands. "Megan, you're pining away for someone who doesn't exist — or who exists only in your imagination. The two of you never even *touched*!"

Well, true.

But. And this is also true. When he looked at me that last day and held my gaze, it was as if the rules of the world shifted. Now, I'm not a New Age-y kind of girl, and it embarrasses me when my boss, Donna, who's a little flaky, uses terms like "astral energy" and "soulscape" and "the interconnectedness of all humanity." I *want* to believe in that stuff; it just sounds hokey.

And yet, the particles in the air changed when Pete and I locked eyes. It was like a jolt of recognition. And that's so rare, I think.

I look straight up at the blue sky, that blinding blue you only see on hot summer days. I lose myself in it. I think about how vast the world is, and how here I am, just a speck in a pool. Maybe it's because I've just graduated and everyone's going their own way and next fall I'll start my freshman year of college, a prospect which both terrifies and thrills me. . . . Maybe that's why I'm suddenly hit with melancholy when moments ago I was feeling so hopeful. All of those farewells, along with the unspoken and unwanted farewell to Pete.

But the sun is shining and, for heaven's sake, it's my birthday. In some ways it's a curse to be born on the Fourth of July, because of the endless and predictable remarks about what a little firecracker I am — especially since I'm not. I would be the most pitiful firecracker ever. I'd shoot into the air and just . . . turn into a marshmallow or something. So anticlimactic. Or I wouldn't even go up in the air. I'd make a *ploof* sound and send up gray smoke from the ground. A dud.

But it's not as if I can change the date of my birth and, anyway, there are some things about it that are really nice. This evening, our whole family will have a picnic at Chastain Park and watch the fireworks display together: Mom, Dad, Aunt Sophie, Uncle Frank, Porter Ann, and me. And our relatives from Alpharetta. And my mom's mom from Decatur, who we call "Sexy Granny" because she wears outrageous wrap dresses involving gold lamé.

Our family always celebrates the Fourth of July at Chastain — along with half the population of Atlanta — and even though it won't be wildly exciting, I know it'll be a good time. When I was little, I thought the festivities were all for me. The noise of the explosions scared me, and I didn't like the burnt smell in the air, and once an ash landed in my eye and made me howl. But I remember gazing out at the hundreds of people and feeling incredibly special.

And then I turned five, and Porter Ann burst my bubble. She informed me that no, the fireworks were actually in celebration of our *country*'s birth, not mine. And by the way, Santa Claus was a phony, as was the Easter Bunny. And seriously, what kind of fairy would collect *teeth*? Fakes, fakes, all fakes. Just a fantasy. Nothing real.

I was heartbroken at the news. I also felt incredibly dumb.

Porter Ann often made me feel that way . . . in fact, sometimes she still does. She's not trying to be malicious. She just can't help herself. She sees me as a skittish kitten — which, face it, I am — while she's saucy and sassy and full of spirit. Porter Ann's the brave one, while I hang back and whisper things like, "Um, I really don't think we should."

But even scaredy-cats have their dreams. And now my mind floats into treacherous territory because here is mine: I'm at Chastain watching the fireworks with my family, and Pete shows up, just randomly. It's a lot to ask, to be given a second chance . . . but this *is* my fantasy. Surely I get to be bold in my own fantasy, even if I'm the opposite of bold in my normal life?

In my daydream, our eyes meet through the crowd and *bang,* we're reconnected. There *is* something between us. I didn't make it up. He makes his way through the crowd to reach me, and my body hums in a way that says, *Yes, this boy is real. And what I'm feeling is real. And it sounds like a fairy tale, but it's not, because when two people fit, that's all there is to it.*

A pang stabs my heart, and I add a crucial detail: *And this time, I swear, I won't run away.*

"Hey! Megan!"

My float up-ends, and I go under. I push to the surface, my hair in ropey clumps over my face, and just like that, I'm back in cold, wet reality.

7

"Porter Ann!" I cry. I go back under and come up right this time, head tilted so that my hair slicks out behind me.

"Sorry," Porter Ann calls from her float. "It's that bathing suit! I couldn't help myself!" She's glam in her white string bikini and big, dark sunglasses, while I'm plain Jane in my plum one-piece. Porter Ann says it's the color of a bruise.

I wave my hand at her, meaning, "Just don't." I've heard it all before: how I'm wasting my cute figure by not wearing more fashionable/flattering/trendy clothes. How my haircut is all wrong (or rather, my lack of a haircut, since I wear my brown hair long and straight and always have). Nice eyes (big and dark), but what a difference it would make if I'd just wear eyeliner! And lipstick!

"I'm not talking fire-engine red here," Porter Ann'll say. "Just gloss! Nice, simple gloss! Could you at least try that?"

She doesn't even have to utter these words because they still echo in my brain. That's how many times we've had this conversation. Her favorite method of attack? "Megan, you are *so* gorgeous — even if you refuse to believe it. Would you let me make you up, just once? *Please?*"

As if the "you're so gorgeous" line — blatantly untrue — would butter me up so much that I'd let her have her way with me. Not going to happen. Skittish kitties don't wear makeup.

*Meow.*

"Don't you flutter your fingers at me," Porter Ann says. "I

have something to say, and I want you to listen. And it goes beyond your bathing suit, hideous as it is."

I arch one eyebrow. "Yes?"

She paddles closer. Her legs are tan and strong. "You are my best and favorite cousin," she says. "'Kay?"

"'Kay," I agree. She's my best and favorite cousin, too, even though she's a nut.

"And blah, blah, blah," she continues, "maybe I should have told you earlier, but I didn't, so too bad. Not about being my favorite cousin, which you already know. But about this."

"About what?"

"Tonight."

"What about tonight?"

She huffs. "Will you just be patient? God!"

I close my eyes. Whatever it is she has up her sleeve, I wish she'd spit it out already. Probably she wants us to slip away from our parents like we did last year. We watched the fireworks from out on the golf course, while she snuck sips of apricot brandy from her cute silver hip flask. I remember how sweet the grass smelled.

"Here's the thing," Porter Ann says. Her voice has that particular *Porter Ann* edge to it, energized and yet slightly antagonistic, as if she expects me to protest and is determined to ride right over it. "I know you think we're going to Chastain, but we're not. I refuse to let you spend your eighteenth birthday with the fam."

9

I groan. This is what she bursts forth with, after all that build-up? Of course we're going to Chastain. We always go to Chastain.

"Well, thanks for your concern," I say. "But I don't mind hanging out with the fam. I like the fam. Anyway, Mom's already packed the —"

"Nope."

"— with hot dogs —"

"Nope."

"— and corn! Corn on the cob!"

"Megan. No. You need to have some fun, and fun does not consist of going on a picnic with Sexy Granny. Go ahead and accept it, because that's the way it is."

I wade through the shallow end, turn around, and hop backward onto the edge. Porter Ann hates it when I do this, because it makes my bathing suit bottom nubbly.

"I've got to go," I say. "Mom's picking me up at four."

"Now, see," Porter Ann says, "this is your problem. You're eighteen, you're starting college in one month — one month! — and you've got to go because your mommy's coming. Which, if you were listening, sweetie, you'd know she's not."

"Yeah, yeah, yeah. Whatever."

"She's not," Porter Ann says. "She's gone far, far away, and she's left you in my care."

"Please," I say. Any moment, Mom and Aunt Sophie will

pull up in the driveway with two-bite brownies and the special potato salad my dad likes, and Mom and I will climb into her Volvo and zoom off to our picnic. With corn on the cob. Which I really do like very much.

I head for the poolhouse.

"Wait!" Porter Ann cries.

I turn around.

"Fine, she hasn't gone far, far away," Porter Ann says.

"Uh-huh," I say.

"But I'm serious, she's not coming to pick you up. She and my mom are going straight to Chastain from the grocery store. Our dads are meeting them there after their golf game."

At first I thought she was yanking my chain, but now I'm genuinely confused — and her expression is making me nervous. She's lowered her sunglasses and is gazing at me over the frames. Her smile says *I know something you don't.*

And come to think of it, Mom *was* acting kind of weird when she and Aunt Sophie left for Whole Foods. She was all, "Happy birthday, sweetie. I love you so much," even though she usually saved her birthday mushiness until she brought out my cake at the park. And she made a point of telling me to be careful, which was unnecessary, since I've been swimming since I was three. Unless she was talking about something else?

Porter Ann slips off her float, dives underwater, and pops up by the edge. She climbs out and shakes herself like a puppy, purposely getting me all wet again. The smell of her coconut sunscreen makes my nose itch.

"Perhaps you're thinking, 'All right, fine, we'll drive to Chastain ourselves,'" she says. "But you would be oh-so-wrong. And would you like to know why?"

"Um . . ."

"Because," she says — pregnant pause — "we have passes to Magnolia."

"No way," I say.

"Way," she says.

"No *way*," I say. My breathing is doing something funny in my chest, and it's not excitement. It should be excitement — any normal girl would be crazy excited — but what I'm feeling is stomach-clenching anxiety.

Magnolia is a hot new club in Buckhead, which is the ritz-iest part of Atlanta, and this evening is to be its spifftacular launch. The radio DJs have been touting its treehouse lounge and rope hammocks and retractable ceiling that slides open on nice nights, so that club-goers can see the stars. And tonight, I suppose, the fireworks.

"My dad got the passes from his law partner, whose client is one of the club's owners," Porter Ann tells me. "And I begged your mom and begged her some more — and finally she said yes!"

She squeals and grabs my hands, no longer teasing me but just being spazzy and happy.

"She did?" I say.

"She did!"

"Omigosh," I say. I've never been to a club. Clubs scare me. I'm horrible at small talk, and I know I'd be too shy to get out on the dance floor and go crazy like Porter Ann. "Ass songs," she calls the fast tracks and, boy, does she know how to shake it. It's like dirty dancing multiplied by . . . well . . . infinity.

I'm trying to get my head around these new birthday plans, and I can't. So I stall.

"What about drinking?" I ask. "Wasn't my mom worried about us drinking?" I'm an only child, so Mom's incredibly overprotective. I really can't believe she told Porter Ann I could go.

"I told her it's an eighteen-and-over club, but to drink you have to have a bracelet," Porter Ann says. "She was, like, 'A *bracelet?*' I had to explain the whole deal to her."

She means the deal of how you have to be twenty-one to get a certain colored bracelet, which tells the bartender it's okay to serve you. I only know this because Porter Ann has led a much more adventurous life than I have, and she shares all the details with me. I also know that Porter Ann's fake ID will score her a bracelet, no problem. But I don't own a fake, so as far as I'm concerned, she was telling Mom the truth.

"What about curfew?" I ask.

"Oh my *God*," Porter Ann says. "Your mom is psycho

13

about that! She wanted you home by twelve, can you believe that? She treats you like you're in kindergarten!"

Okay, first of all, Porter Ann doesn't need to tell me that Mom is psycho about my curfew. I actually already know that, just as I know that the day I miss curfew is the day I can say bye-bye to what little freedom I have.

And second, I don't know of a single kindergartner who's allowed to stay out till midnight. Not even Jolene Fitzhugh from down the street, whose mother lets her eat Splenda.

"But I told her the fireworks there don't even *start* till twelve," Porter Ann barrels on, "so she relented and said you could stay out until twelve thirty. Because, you know, that's what a big person she is. Still, the point is you can go!"

I blink.

Porter Ann's bouncing up and down. It takes her a second to realize I'm not. Then she gets a threatening expression on her face — very firm and *I know what's best for you* — and says, "Megan . . . don't you *want* to go?"

I try to figure out what's going on inside of me, other than normal Megan wimpiness. Because I do want to go, kind of. I *want* to want to.

But if I do, it'll mean giving up my Pete-in-the-park fantasy. Oh God, is that what's holding me back? It's like I've decided in my head that I'm going to see him tonight, and I'm not willing to shift gears. How pathetic is that?

"You're thinking about Pete, aren't you?" Porter Ann accuses.

I start. How did she know?

"I can read it in your face," she says. "You're thinking about Pete, and you probably have this whole elaborate fantasy of how the two of you are going to meet up under the stars." She widens her eyes. "Omigod! You do! Megan, that's so adorably sad!"

This is the problem with best and favorite cousins. They know you far too well.

"What's even sadder is that even if you *did* run into him under the stars, you wouldn't do anything. Would you?"

"I would so," I say.

"Mmm-hmm, yeah, right."

"I would!"

"Okay, let's consider it another way. He's just as likely to show up at Magnolia as he is at Chastain. What if he shows up at Magnolia, huh? And you're there, too. Will you do something then?"

"He's not going to show up at Magnolia," I say, as if she's now the one spinning unrealistic fantasies. It's horrible and awful talking about this out loud, and it makes me feel stupid.

"I'm just saying," she says. "Look me straight in the eye and swear to me that if by some crazy twist of fate you do see

Pete tonight — I don't care where — then you'll *do* something about it. Something more than gazing at him from the corner of your eye and sighing."

Curse best and favorite cousins.

"Swear it," she says. "Or I'll totally hate you, because I'll know you'd rather be ruled by fear than take the plunge and control your own life."

"Porter Ann . . ."

"Maybe I won't *hate* you," she tempers. "But I'll pity you and mock you and never invite you anywhere again."

"Promise?"

"Ha-ha."

My face is hot, but she's not letting me off the hook. She's staring at me, waiting for me to swear, and I'm about to pull a typical Megan move and shut down, telling myself it's because she's being a jerk and not because she's found the rawest spot inside of me and is holding it up to the light. I'll drive myself to Chastain. She can go to Magnolia on her own.

Then something deep inside me speaks up, deeper than fear and embarrassment and shame at being such a wimp. And what this gut-level part of me says is, *Come on, Megan.* Meaning, rise to the challenge. Deal with it. Stop living in la-la-land.

Pete isn't going to magically appear and come back into my life, whether at the park *or* the club. I wish things would happen just because people want them to, but they don't.

Which leaves me with two options: I can float through life having wistful daydreams, or I can admit that I had my chance and blew it. And decide to move on.

"Megan?" Porter Ann says. Even though she's playing hardball, I can tell she's slightly worried.

"Why did you wait so long to invite me?" I finally ask.

"I didn't want you to have time to back out, if you agreed to go." She quickly corrects herself. "*When* you agree to go."

I take a breath. "All right."

"All right *what*? You'll go? Or all right, you swear you'll jump Pete's bones if you run into him?"

She just won't give up, will she?

"Both," I say. "Well, not jump his bones, because some of us are a little classier than that."

She jabs me hard in the ribs. I laugh, and it's good to have the yuckiness between us blow away.

"Yes," I say. "*If* I see Pete, which I won't, I promise I'll actually *do* something about it. Are you satisfied?"

"Yay!" she says. "Yay, yay, yay!" She throws her arms around me, and we stumble backward.

When she releases me, she's a ball of determination. She says, "Change into dry clothes and get your fanny in the Saab — I want to make it to the club by seven." She claps, two staccato bursts. "Chop-chop! Time's a-wasting!"

"Are you on drugs?" I say. "It's only three forty-five."

"Yes, and I've booked you for a makeover at four fifteen,"

she replies. A smile stretches across her face. "You, my dear cousin, are going to be transformed."

At Buzz and Bumble, a full-service salon that Porter Ann claims is "the finest in the city," I wipe my sweaty palms on my shorts as Porter Ann confers with the stylist and "aesthetician." My hair is freshly shampooed, leaving wet splotches on my black cape, and I glance away when I catch a glimpse of myself in the mirror. I've decided that if I'm doing this, I should do it all the way. But I'm having a hard time breathing normally. I keep telling myself, *Relax, just relax.*

Still. Even though I'm nervous, I'm exhilarated, too. Porter Ann lives in a different world than I do — a kingdom of full-service salons and Saabs and backyard pools — and I can't help but feel giddy getting a taste of it. She has a Platinum Visa and the statements go straight to Uncle Stuart's automated payment plan. She's informed me that we're to knock ourselves out or he'll be extremely disappointed. I love that, that he's so generous. I would be, too — I hope — if I were rich.

Uncle Stuart comes from "old money," that's what Mom calls it. Supposedly, when my aunt Sophie first married him, she felt uncomfortable with her new wealth. She's since gotten over it. They live in Ansley Park instead of Smyrna, and they have a maid named Dolly who folds Porter Ann's thongs and handwashes her Le Mystère demi-bras from Paris. Dolly also irons Porter Ann's endless tanks, hoodies, boxers, and sweats, all emblazoned with the Greek letters for Alpha Pi Omega, the University of Georgia's top-tiered sorority.

There's another bizarre and almost incomprehensible world that Porter Ann has introduced me to: UGA's Greek system. Porter Ann called me the night she received her bid from the Alpha Pi's, and for the longest time, I couldn't understand her, because she was crying so hard. I thought she was disappointed until she hiccupped and said, "No! I'm just so happy! I always wanted a sister, and now I have two hundred!"

As the semester progressed, and as Porter Ann's life was taken over with pledge activities, she stopped calling as often as she used to. When she did call, all she talked about was Alpha Pi. She colored her hair a paler shade of blond, because that was the Alpha Pi look. She became one of those girls who talked about calories and obsessed about getting her workout in every day. She started throwing in remarks about girls from other sororities that seemed unnecessarily mean.

Some of the Alpha Pi activities she told me about sounded fun, like the midnight all-you-can-eat pancake buffet the girls hosted, with the profits going to some charity or another. Porter Ann wasn't sure which. But some of the stuff seemed sexist and wrong, like the time her whole pledge class had to scrub the floor of the Alpha Pi dining room with toothbrushes, wearing only their bras and undies. Can anyone say "hazing"?

But she didn't want to hear it when I suggested as much,

and I stopped wanting to hear about how the Alpha Pis did this or her Alpha Pi sisters thought that. It seemed like they were taking the Porter Ann I knew and turning her into someone else.

Or maybe I was just jealous. I had always thought of *myself* as kind of like Porter Ann's sister.

But then she came back to Atlanta for summer break, and at first it was weird between us, but slowly she morphed back into the same bossy, shocking, bighearted Porter Ann I'd grown up with. And then one night she told me how glad she was to be home, and how it was so much harder than she'd expected to march off to college and pretend to be having the time of her life.

"I mean, I like being an Alpha Pi, don't get me wrong," she said. I was sleeping over, and we were lying in the dark, talking in that real way that happens when you can't see each other's faces. "And I don't want you taking this as, like, ammunition. Because I know you're not a fan."

I waited.

"It's just that sometimes I felt like I was playing a role," she confessed. "Like, *look at me, I'm such a crazy-ass! I'm laughing hysterically with my sorority sisters!* When the real me would have rather been in my dorm room, watching the *Gilmore Girls* in my PJs. You know?"

I was so surprised to hear her admit that. And then I wasn't, remembering how uncharacteristically catty she'd become for a while there. Snobby, too, like making fun of another girl by suggesting her necklace came out of a quarter machine at Kmart. My general assumption is that when someone acts like that, they can't be very happy.

Still, it was one of those mind-blowing realizations that even someone as sure of herself as Porter Ann — someone I saw as *oozing* with self-confidence — could fall into the trap of being overly influenced by others. I thought about that deep into the night, long after Porter Ann fell asleep, because of course I knew what it was like to worry too much about what people might think. I do that all the time. The world is huge. It seems so easy to make a wrong step.

That night, in Porter Ann's bedroom, I wanted to wake her up and give her a hug and watch an episode of the *Gilmore Girls* with her then and there. And in fact, I rented the first season's DVD the next day, and we watched it that weekend. She wore boxers and a T-shirt instead of her pink Alpha Pi jammies, which I noticed but didn't mention.

Maybe, it occurs to me in the salon, that's why the Pete thing pushed her buttons so much. Because she hated seeing me not follow my heart, so soon after her return from a tough year at college where she was having a hard time following her *own* heart. That would be kind of cool, if my helping her be more true to herself led to her wanting to do the same for me.

Over by the receptionist's desk, Porter Ann's high-pitched squeal jerks me out of my reverie.

"Yes, yes, yes!" she exclaims. "That's *exactly* what I had in mind!"

I gulp as she and the two beauty professionals march over. Raoul, the stylist, takes me by the shoulders and leads me to his station. He rubs my muscles as we walk.

"You trust Raoul, okay?" he says in a heavily accented voice. "Raoul make you look *fab*-oo-lous. Turn ugly duckling into flan."

I stumble. Did he just call me an ugly duckling? And then suggest he'd turn me into *flan*, the brown-sugar custard I order at La Fonda Latina?

"*Swan*," says Amber, the aesthetician. She rolls her eyes. "Suh-*wan*."

Raoul waves his hand in the air. "Flan, swan . . . *pffff*." He eases me into the chair. "You want tea? Coca-cola?"

"No thanks," I say and immediately regret it. I *would* like a Coke, although it's too late to backtrack. Why do I always say "no" to things I actually want?

Raoul lifts a lock of my damp hair as if weighing it, and Amber peers at my skin. She asks whether I prefer a natural look or something more dramatic, and when I say "natural," Porter Ann blows out a puff of air.

"Uh, dra*mat*ic," she says, looking at Amber as if to say, *Haven't we gone over this?*

"It's my birthday," I tell Amber apologetically. "Porter Ann's taking me to Magnolia."

22

"You're going to Magnolia?" she exclaims. "My girlfriend's been trying for weeks to get us passes!"

"My daddy's law partner knows the owner," Porter Ann says.

"Then dramatic it is," Amber tells me. "One last question: What length lash extensions do you want?"

"Lash extensions?" I repeat.

Porter Ann taps her finger against her full lower lip. "Let's go with eleven and thirteen."

"Eleven and thirteen *what*?" I say.

"Centimeters," Amber replies. To Porter Ann, she says, "Black?"

"As night," Porter Ann says. And grins.


Two hours later, I'm a new person. Seriously, I'm not me anymore — or at least that's the way it feels. I'm no longer Megan Meyers but some gorgeous creature who, if I ran into myself on the street, I would be thoroughly intimidated by. In a *good* way . . . but still. I'm normally not the type of girl who would intimidate anyone.

My hair, formerly a wavy brown mess, now cascades around my face like a supermodel's. Raoul razor-cut it to make it less heavy, then gave me a deep side part to create swoopy bangs. I've always wanted swoopy bangs, the sort that slide glamorously over one eye. After straightening the longer sections of my hair with his hot iron, he showed me how to take a

23

dollop of shine enhancer, rub it between my palms, and "clap" it on, pulling down hard for maximum sheen. When I shake my head, the strands catch the light like spun glass.

As for my face . . . wow. Amber is a miracle worker. She claimed the basic elements were already there, praising my peaches-and-cream complexion and pixie-like features, but come on. I have never looked this frickin' good in my life.

Shimmery blush gives me a dewy glow, and a lip-tint-plus-gloss makes my mouth look stained by raspberry juice. My mahogany eyes are lined with aubergine eyeliner, which I've never used before, and it's amazing how huge they appear. Of course, that's also due to the lash extensions, which are phe-nomenal. Amber had me lie still while she applied them, eyes closed, and because I didn't feel anything, I didn't predict the magnitude of the final effect.

"There," she said, after affixing the final lash. She had me sit up and handed me a mirror. "What do you think?"

I gazed at myself, speechless. My eyelashes were so long they fluttered against my brow bone when I blinked. For real. But they didn't look fake or costume-y; they were soft and nat-ural, curling upward in a soft arc.

"How long will they last?" I asked, entranced by my reflection.

"Two to four weeks," Amber told me. "But you've got to be gentle with them. No rubbing, and no oil-based makeup remover. Most important, don't get them wet."

"Ever?" I asked, wondering how I'd wash my face.

"Just for tonight. After that, I still don't want you using oil-based products, but otherwise you can follow your normal beauty routine."

*My beauty routine,* I thought. *Um, yeah.*

While Raoul and Amber worked their magic on my hair and face, Porter Ann had ducked out of the salon to scour the racks of the nearby boutiques. She returned laden with bags, the contents of which she insisted I try on in the Buzz and Bumble changing room.

That's what I'm doing now.

She's gone overboard, as usual, and as I slip my feet into the sandals she's chosen, I feel amazingly grateful. And a little overwhelmed because it's too much, it really is, and I know I can never return the favor, at least not in a money, gift-giving way. But I remind myself that Porter Ann's doing this because she wants to. She's like my trendy fairy godmother.

"Come on, come on," Porter Ann calls from outside the changing room. "Stop stalling, you sexy beast!"

I open the door to a collective gasp. Porter Ann has always made fun of me for wearing black so much, which I wear not to be Goth but because it's easy and doesn't draw attention. To force me out of my rut, for tonight she's chosen a silk slip dress in lemony yellow. I've always been embarrassed that I don't have much of a bust, but the cut of this dress makes me look slender and waifish rather than skinny and flat. I'm tan from my afternoons at Porter Ann's pool, and the play of yellow against golden brown helps me realize that any body type can work in the right outfit. I feel like I've wasted eighteen years being frumpy, when all along I could have been so much more.

My delicate open-toed sandals show off my freshly painted toenails, and five metallic bangles jangle on my wrist. Porter Ann's always on me to wear more jewelry, and maybe she's right. Looking so fancy makes me want to twirl, so I do.

"*Fab*-oo-lous," Raoul declares, clasping his hands to his heart.

"You will never look lovelier than you look right now," Amber says earnestly. I hope that's not true — I mean, God, how depressing to peak at eighteen — but even so, I bask in her approval.

"Remember to keep those eyes dry," she warns. She grooms one wayward lash.

"I will," I promise.

Porter Ann beams. She hugs me from behind, our eyes meeting in the mirror.

"Baby," she says, "you are *flan*."

It's twilight when we leave the salon, and I feel disoriented, like when you enter a movie theater in bright sunlight and come out after dark. We get wolf whistles from some guys across the street, and Porter Ann flips them the bird.

"Rednecks," she says.

"Oh, please, you love it," I say. "Anyway, you can't wear a dress like that and not be whistled at!"

Porter Ann grins. Her new dress is true red, and its halter-style top covers her nipples, but little more. "Side cleavage," she bragged when she emerged from the salon's changing room.

Her Saab is at the far end of the parking lot. The setting sun warms my bare arms and as I walk, my bracelets tinkle.

"Porter Ann . . . thank you," I say.

"Of course," she says.

"No, really. Thank you."

"You're very welcome," she says. "And now your only job is to have fun. Got it?"

We park two blocks away from the club, across from a small neighborhood playground, because Porter Ann wants to do a little pre-gaming away from the prying eyes of the bouncers. "Pre-gaming" is a sorority term for getting tipsy before an event, so that by the time you arrive, you're already giddy and giggly and flirty as hell.

I'm not interested in getting tipsy, but the night is beautiful, and the breeze drifting through our open windows smells like magnolia blossoms, sweet and lush. Which is perfect, given where we're headed. I love the smell of magnolias.

I read somewhere that you can never escape your childhood home, that where you grow up stays inside of you forever.

I know that's true for me. The South isn't perfect, no place is, but I went to Wyoming once with my parents, and all I could think was, *Whoa, it's so dry. And dusty. And the colors are so pale*! It was an interesting landscape, very cowboy-y and wild wild west, but I felt as if, at any moment, a fierce wind might catch me up and blow me away. I missed Atlanta's trees. I needed them to hold me down.

There are plenty of trees here at the park, and one of them, a sprawling oak, casts evening shadows over three little girls on a tire swing. The swing is one where the tire hangs horizontally and you dangle your feet through the middle, and I ask Porter Ann if she remembers what we used to call that type of swing.

"Uh . . . a tire swing?" she says.

I swat her, because she *does* remember. I know she does.

"No, a potty swing," I say. "You'd spin around and pretend you were being flushed down, down, down. You'd be like, 'Oh no! Into the sewer!'"

Porter Ann laughs. She's halfway through her flask of Bacardi, so she's an easy mark.

"Here," she says, passing me the rum. I wet my lips, then pass back the flask.

"Mmm," Porter Ann says now, resting her head against the headrest. "You couldn't ask for better Fourth of July weather."

"So true," I say. Although come to think of it, I'm actually a little hot. Of course it's Atlanta, and it's going to be hot . . . but my thighs are sticking to the seat. I hope I'm not wrinkling my dress.

Porter Ann lolls her head toward me. "That color looks amazing on you," she says. "You're like an M&M. A yellow M&M."

"Which is so incredibly lucky, because that's just the look I'm going for," I say.

"Ah," Porter Ann says. "Hope you don't melt."

If this heat keeps up, I surely will. I shift in my seat.

"So. Meg-Meg. I need to tell you something," Porter Ann says.

"Shoot."

"It's more like a confession, really. But I don't want you to freak out, 'kay?"

I give her a look. She's not allowed to say that, and she knows it. We've talked about how unfair it is to say, "I don't want you to freak out" or "Don't be mad" right before dropping a bombshell.

"What is it?" I say.

"Um, first let me ask you this. With Pete, and your whole crush/obsession thing . . ."

I feel myself blush. Why is she bringing this up again?

"Well, what if he *didn't* feel the earth move the way you did?"

"I never said the earth moved," I protest.

29

"Okay, *but*. You felt this big connection; it was like a religious experience for you —"

"Not a religious experience! Please stop taking this and making it sound so stupid!"

"— and I'm just wondering if you've ever considered the possibility that for him, it wasn't. I mean, could you handle that? If you saw him again and he didn't remember you?"

"Of course I could handle it," I say defensively. I'm not an idiot. And yet her words make me feel faint. It must be the heat, that's why I'm reacting this way.

"I mean, if he saw you tonight, looking like this, he wouldn't even recognize you."

"He would," I insist. "I know he would." I fan myself and unstick my thighs *again*, and a tiny red light on the dashboard catches my eye. The seat warmer. Porter Ann turned on my seat warmer — that's why I'm so frickin' hot.

"Dammit, Porter Ann!" I say. I jab the button, and she breaks into peals of laughter.

"I put you on the hot seat!" she crows.

"Very funny." My parents' Chevy doesn't have seat warmers. No other car I've ever been in has seat warmers. But the Saab is fully loaded — just like Porter Ann.

"I put you on the hot seat," she repeats, all singsongy.

"*Why?*" I demand. "And why are you making me think about Pete when I'd finally managed to put him out of my mind?"

She waves her hand. "You hadn't put him out of your mind. Don't give me that."

I get a bad feeling as I put together her Pete questions with her warning that she had a "confession" to make. "Porter Ann? Would you please tell me what it is you need to confess? As in, right this very second?"

Her cell rings, and she fishes it out of her purse. She flips it open and says, "Oooh, hold that thought. *Very* important call." She angles it toward me so I can read the name on the screen — *Meredith* — then presses the answer button and says, "Hey, bay-bay. 'Sup?"

Meredith, I recall, is a fellow Alpha Pi, and Porter Ann becomes immediately engrossed in whatever Meredith's telling her.

"He is?" Porter Ann says. "You're sure? You're absolutely, positively sure?"

I sigh, assuming she's in for a chat. God, that girl is aggravating. And what is the confession she needs to make? With Porter Ann, it could be anything. I could be right to be worried, or it could end up being nothing. But why the grand inquisition about Pete?

I lean forward and gaze at myself in the side mirror, propping my forearms on the open window and my chin on my arms. *Would he really not recognize me?* I wonder. *Is it possible that what I thought was real never was?*

Well, he's back in my mind now — thanks, Porter

Ann — so I decide to indulge myself, even though I know it's foolish. *What the hell*, I say to myself, and I let myself remember that wonderful week.

I was working at the preschool, where I have a summer job teaching the Head Start kids. It was swelteringly hot, because the air conditioner was broken. Pete's dad was the technician who diagnosed the problem. Pete was the guy who did the actual fixing.

I was taken with him from the moment I saw him, and not just because he was heartstoppingly cute, although he was. He had military-short hair, which normally I don't like, but which on him accentuated the strength of his features. Square jaw. Amazing brown eyes. And a frickin' amazing body, all tan arms and firm muscles under the adorable blue-and-white-striped work shirt he wore, which said TRANE AIR CONDITIONING on the left pocket.

He was gorgeous. I admit it. But what captured my heart was seeing the way he interacted with the kids, who were awe-struck by this fascinating "worker guy," as they called him, who came into their midst and disrupted their normal schedule. They didn't want any more circle time; they wanted to watch Pete pry off the metal grates that led to the air ducts. They had no interest in their rainbow-colored goldfish and apple juice; they only wanted to follow Pete around the building and admire his tools.

Well, who could blame them? I did, too.

Donna, the lead teacher in our classroom, said that Pete had "good energy." I wholeheartedly agreed. She said his aura was blue, indicating strength of character and a gentle spirit and, again, I gave her assessment a big thumbs-up. She also pulled me aside and whispered that he would be a perfect match for me, as our chakras were in alignment. I blushed and developed a sudden need to straighten up the alphabet blocks. I didn't know what "chakras" were, but I did know that when it came to his, I'd very much like to find out.

In the middle of the week, a four-year-old named Manuel pulled a disappearing act. This was bad: A childcare facility is not supposed to lose its charges. But Manuel was an adorable scamp, and this wasn't the first time he'd managed to sneak out of the room while Donna and I were focused on other kids. We searched all of Manuel's usual haunts — the snack closet, the row of pre-K-sized water fountains, the teacher's bathroom with the yummy smelling squirt-soap — but he was nowhere to be found.

Donna paced in her flowy tie-dye dress. "I don't think he's hurt," she said. "I would sense it if he were. But where *is* he?"

Right about then, Pete appeared in our doorway, his strong, capable hand on Manuel's shoulder. "Found this little guy in the crawl space," he said.

"No!" Donna said. She knelt by Manuel. "Manuel, you know you're not allowed in the crawl space!"

"Nuh-uh," Manuel said. "That's not one of the rules." He ticked them off on his fingers. "Take care of ourselves. Take care of our friends. Take care of our things. You never said anything about crawling spaces!"

Pete laughed. He looked at me, not Donna, and said, "Humans sure are funny, aren't they?"

*Those* were my six words. I giggled and said something brilliant like, "Uh-huh."

I liked it that he found the situation funny rather than annoying. Not all "worker guys" would have handled a preschooler in the crawl space as graciously. I also liked it that he said humans were funny, not kids. I don't know why exactly, just that it hinted at a world view that I appreciated. Humans *were* funny. All of us, Pete and I included.

It was because of that comment, and the way he directed it just at me, that I felt pretty sure he noticed me as a girl and not just as the assistant preschool teacher in the building whose air conditioner was shot. Also because of the way I'd felt his eyes on me when I read *Knuffle Bunny* for story time, or when I helped everyone make pinecone owls with orange felt beaks.

I wanted him to do something about it, but he didn't. After all, we were both working. It's not like we were ever alone. And despite the ease he displayed with pressure gauges and screwdrivers, I got the sense that he was shy, too. Like me.

Then, on the last day Pete was there, we ran into each

other in the hall. Just the two of us. I'd slipped out of the room to get some antibacterial soap from the supply closet, and I can't be sure, but I couldn't help wondering if maybe Pete had seen me leave and had engineered an errand to run himself.

I stopped short and smiled at him. He smiled, too. I knew one of us was supposed to be saying something, that's the way it's supposed to work, but I was so fully immersed in the moment of soaking him in, there in the hall, that the thought of words just didn't bubble into my brain. I'd heard of "chemistry" all my life, that undeniable attraction between two people, but I'd assumed it was the lore of the dog-eared romance paperbacks I read at the beach. Either that, or that chemistry, like so many other things, was for other people, not me.

But I could *feel* Pete's presence, even though we weren't touching. His body heat sent sparks up and down my skin. We gazed at each other, and no, the earth didn't move, but yes, something inside of him met with something inside of me. And yes, it felt like magic.

And then Donna stuck her head out of the room and said, "Megan! Grab me a Pull-Up. We have an emergency!" Which pretty much ended the moment. I jumped and scurried down the hall, and Pete went back to doing whatever he was doing.

That afternoon, he screwed the last grate back in place and told Donna he was heading out. I was washing paintbrushes in the sink at the time and though I wanted to turn around, I didn't. Because I'm a wimp. But before his truck pulled out of the parking lot, Donna realized he'd forgotten his chrome lunch box.

"Here, Megan, run this out to him," she said.

I took it, but I didn't move.

"He left it on purpose!" she said. "Like when a girl leaves her purse in a boy's car, so that the boy has to go back to her house. He wants a minute alone with you, Megan! Go!"

Still, I stood there. My stomach tightened, and my palm on the lunch box handle grew sweaty. This is what happens when I want something: I freeze, or say no, or scurry away. Why? I don't know! Because I get scared? Because wanting something is easier than actually going for it? Because it's hard to step forward and *act* when you're used to hiding out on the sidelines?

Manuel snatched the lunch box away from me. "I'll take it," he said, and off he dashed.

"Manuel!" Donna called.

It was too late. From the window, we watched Manuel pop out of the back door and hand Pete his lunch box. Pete ruffled Manuel's hair and then, with one last glance at the building, he drove away.

Porter Ann's wrapping up her conversation with Meredith, so I shake myself out of my memories and make an effort to focus on what's around me. Porter Ann, who's saying, "Okay, sweetie, I'll talk to you then." The leather seat under my thighs, no longer toasty warm. The little girls on the tire swing, swirling like drunken fairies.

"So what's up with Meredith?" I ask after Porter Ann snaps her phone shut.

She grins, very Cheshire-Cat-ish. "She was just confirming that yes, a certain Trane employee named Pete will indeed be at Magnolia tonight."

"*What?!*" I screech. Oh God, oh God. Sudden hyperventilation. "But how would she . . . why would she even . . . you mean *my* Pete? He'll be at Magnolia? *Tonight?*"

"'My Pete,' I love it," Porter Ann says. "That's the confidence you need to channel when you see him, 'kay? Just tell yourself, 'Hey, there's my boy. Pete! Darling! Give me a smooch, you big stud!'"

I grab her wrists to make her quit gesticulating. "Porter Ann. How does Meredith know Pete's going to be there tonight?"

"That's my confession," she says. "See . . . I sort of did some asking around on your behalf."

My heart thumps. There's something balloon-y in my chest, and it might be joy, but it might be terror. "Explain."

Porter Ann frees herself from my death grip. "Well, I know Pete works for Trane, because you told me."

37

"I did?"

She cocks her head. "Uh, yes? Along with every other miniscule detail you managed to wring from y'all's little moment?"

"Oh. Right."

"*And*, Kelsey's uncle happens to work for Trane, too, and as it turns out, Trane's the company that installed the air-conditioning for Magnolia!"

"Who's Kelsey?" I say, baffled.

"Another pledge sister. Once you're in a sorority, it's like that six-degrees-of-separation thing."

"Six degrees of Alpha Pi," I say.

"Uh-huh. So, see? Sororities *do* have their good points!"

"I never said they didn't! Will you please get back to Pete?!"

"Soooo, Meredith's dad is friends with the owner of Magnolia, so Meredith suggested, very politely, that wouldn't it be nice if he comped opening-night passes to the workmen who'd done such a fantastic job bringing everything together. And he did! And according to Kelsey, who talked to her uncle, Pete is definitely planning on going!"

Whoa. My head is spinning. "Pete's going to be there? Tonight?"

"Yeppers." She beams.

"You did all that, talking to Meredith's uncle and Kelsey's dad —"

"*Kelsey*'s uncle. Meredith's dad's *friend*."

"— just to get Pete to Magnolia?"

"For your birthday!" she says. "Happy birthday!"

My breath is short. I feel woozy. But I'm also amazingly touched.

"*Why?*" I say. "Why in the world did you go to so much trouble?"

"Because I wanted to, you doof." She hesitates, and what flickers in her eyes is unexpectedly vulnerable. Like she's letting me see inside of Porter Ann for real, just for this rare moment. "Because you're my best and favorite cousin. And because you rented the *Gilmore Girls* for me."

I get teary, which is crazy. Even crazier, she's teary, too.

"Don't," she commands, pointing at me sternly. "You'll mess up your eyelashes."

"And we can't have that," I say.

One of the little girls struggles off the tire and wobbles toward a green dinosaur on a sturdy metal spring. She falls before she gets there, laughing hysterically.

Porter Ann steps out of the Saab, and I do the same. My legs, like the little girl's, are wobbly.

Porter Ann clicks the LOCK button on her key, and the Saab beeps.

"Come on, muffin," she says, circling the car and looping her arm through mine. "The night of your life awaits."

\* \* \*

Magnolia is magnificent. Twinkle lights beckon us toward the front entrance, where two burly men check IDs and funky jazz cascades over the line of people waiting to go in. The humid air carries the scent of different perfumes, all mingling together. Bare shoulders, bare backs, bare necks — everyone is summer-bronzed and dewy. Everyone is hopeful.

Porter Ann strides to the front of the line. I follow, conscious of my heart, which is drumming beneath my silk yellow dress. I try not to look for Pete. I can't help but look for Pete. Oh my God, what if I really see him? It's extremely possible I'll combust. *Poof.* I'll turn into a marshmallow, and Pete surely won't recognize me then.

Several yards from the bouncers, Porter Ann stops me and says, "Hold on — I've got one last surprise."

*"No!"* I cry. "No more surprises — I can't take it!"

She laughs. "This one's no biggie, I promise. Your purse, my dear?"

"What are you up to?"

She holds out her hand. I hand her my funky embroidered clutch. She confiscates my license from the zippered pocket and replaces it with another. I reclaim my purse and pull out the new ID.

"Ceri-Lune Fornatale?" I read, squinting at the name.

"You're Italian!" Porter Ann crows. "Isn't that brilliant?"

"Porter Ann, I'm not Italian," I say. "I'm also not twenty-one."

"Oh yes you are," she says. She taps the girl in the picture. "She's a dead ringer for you, yeah?"

"Who *is* she?" I ask. Then I answer my own question. "Never mind. An Alpha Pi. But . . . I thought all Alpha Pi's were blond!"

"Stereotype, stereotype, stereotype," she says. "We even have a redhead. We're very diverse."

"You don't say."

"Anyway, her license is yours for tonight, but tomorrow I've got to give it back." She's delighted with herself and wants me to be delighted, too.

"Ceri-Lune," I say, fingering the ID, "such a pretty name."

"Pretty name for a pretty girl," Porter Ann quips.

She prods me toward the beefier of the two bouncers, to whom we present our passes and display our IDs. He gives us blue bracelets with white stars to slip onto our wrists. Mine's loose, and I tilt my arm so it won't fall off. It slides down practically to my elbow. Still, I like the way it looks. The under-twenty-one bracelets are solid red, not nearly as charming.

"Have fun, ladies," the bouncer says, lifting the velvet rope.

"You know it," Porter Ann says.

Drinks are Porter Ann's first order of business. I volunteer to push my way up to the bar, because I'm too jittery to stay in

41

one place. Plus, it'll let me scope the crowd for Pete. The club is packed; it's pulsing with laughter and energy, but all I care about is Pete.

I order a mojito for Porter Ann and a Sprite for me. Maybe I'll get a real drink later, but not yet.

I weave back to Porter Ann, and we clink glasses.

"Happy birthday," she says.

I smile.

"And don't worry, he'll show up."

"If he doesn't, that's okay," I say.

"You are so incredibly full of it," she says, shaking her head. "God knows why, but I love you anyway."

We raise our glasses and drink.

By eleven, Pete still hasn't appeared, and I'm worn out from all the adrenaline I've spent: perking up and getting panicky each time I think I see him, then sinking into disappointment when it's not. I'm a frayed bundle of nerves.

Porter Ann, on the other hand, is a wild woman. She's out on the dance floor twisting and shimmying and shaking her booty, and this one blond guy in particular is entranced. He's tall, with chiseled muscles visible under his crisp dress shirt, which is unbuttoned to his sternum. Handsome — but cheesy. I roll my eyes when Porter Ann giddily informs me that he's a male stripper.

"Porter *Ann*," I say. I'm hanging out on the sidelines, but every couple of songs, Porter Ann finds me and gives me updates.

"His name's Billy Clyde," she says. She giggles. "He thinks I'm something else."

"You *are* something else."

"He has soulful eyes. Don't you think? Don't you think he has soulful eyes?" She loses her balance and falls on me. I prop her back up.

"Got to go, Meggers!" she says. "Ciao!"

I laugh. At least I have her to distract me. But just watching her dance is making me thirsty, and I decide I'm ready for something other than Sprite. Why not? The night has gotten to the point where I feel ready to throw it all to the wind.

I head for the bar, but as I squeeze through to the counter, I realize my rubber bracelet's gone. I look to see where I might have dropped it, but it's way too crowded. I can barely see the floor through the maze of legs and ankles and strappy sandals.

No problem, I'll just use my ID. Again, why not? I have a total "what the hell" attitude — completely foreign to me — and I'm going to go with it. Let whatever happens, happen. I unzip the side pocket of my clutch, trying not to elbow the people around me. Ceri-Lune's license snags on a thread, and when I yank at it, it comes free all at once, flying out of my fingers and sailing in an arc through the air. *Dammit!*

And then.

My heart stops.

Because a guy who looks an awful lot like Pete — although a *lot* of guys have looked like Pete — sticks his hand up and *thwack*, his fingers close around it.

Holy cats, holy cats, holy cats. He's making his way over, angling his hips to squeeze past a woman in black, and it *is* Pete, I'm absolutely sure of it. His shoulders are still broad. His forearms, extending from his cuffed sleeves, are tan and strong. And he looks *really* good in a dress shirt, although he looked really good in his work shirt, too.

I feel lightheaded.

"You could have poked someone's eye out," he says. His smile is just as I remember: shy, but with a hint of a question.

As for me, in his presence, I'm once again speechless. I'm also a sweaty mess. I'm thankful my dress is sleeveless.

He flips the license over and examines it. "Beautiful moon?"

My brain refuses to kick into gear. *Why in heaven's name is he discussing the moon?*

He hands me my ID. "I've never heard that name before. It's different. I like it."

*"Ohhh,"* I say, piecing it together. "Lune" equals "moon," and "Ceri" must mean "beautiful." He's referring to the name on the license. "You speak Italian?"

"Not really," he says.

"Thank God," I say. "I mean . . ." Well, I don't know what I mean. I let it drop and shrug instead, like, *Huh*.

We stare at each other. That undeniable chemistry between us is still there, and I want to ask if he feels it, too. This tingling sensation between us that's making me smile so goofily. But those aren't words I know how to say, especially since I'm not even sure if he recognizes me. He has to, though. Doesn't he?

The pounding music isn't helping. Neither is the sway and buckle of the crowd.

"It's kind of loud in here," I say, just as he says, "Want to go somewhere quieter? Where we can talk?"

We grin.

"Yeah," I say.

He leads me through the throng of partygoers, past the dance floor, and out a back exit. Immediately, the noise diminishes. We can still hear the music, but it's *so* much better. In front of us is a goldfish pond set among large rocks. Honeysuckle twines up a wooden arbor. Crickets chirp, a refreshing sound after the throb of the club.

"Wow," I say. I kick off my sandals and sit on the nearest rock, gingerly dipping one foot into the cool water. It feels great, so I lower my other foot in, as well. "How did you know this place was out here?"

"I did some work on the building when it was being constructed," he says.

"Oh yeah," I say, remembering the whole uncle-dad's-friend–Alpha Pi connection.

He looks puzzled.

I pick up a stick and start fooling with it to hide how stupid I feel.

He drops down beside me on the rock. "The owner gave us passes for tonight, so I thought, 'Why not?'"

I nod, like, *ah*.

We watch the goldfish. They're the lovely big kind, iridescent in the dark pond. I try out phrases in my mind, such as, "I've been hoping to see you," or "I'm sorry I ran off that time in the hall," or "You *do* know I'm actually not Ceri-Lune, but Megan, right? The girl from the preschool?"

Out of all my stilted-sounding phrases, that's the one I need to say. But the longer I wait, the weirder it gets. I *do* look different than my ponytailed preschool teacher self — my hair, my fabulous eyelashes, my dress. But true love's supposed to see past all that, isn't it?

*True love?* What am I doing thinking such words? And I'm not even drunk.

He tells me how he grew up on his family's farm, not too far from here in Lawrenceville, and how he was always tinkering with tools and machinery. Then his dad sold the farm and took a job with Trane, and Pete signed on for the summer to get "real world" experience. But the city is bigger than he thought, and he's felt kind of lost since he's been here.

I tell him I know what that's like, because I almost always feel that way. Lost. As if other people have a "navigating-the-world" gene that I just don't possess. It's amazing to be talking to another human being about this.

"And at shopping malls?" I say, after having told him about the claustrophobia I feel in airports. "I stand there sometimes, watching all the people. And I *like* them, I feel fond of them as a species, but sometimes I feel like they're hurrying off to a specific destination, while I'm just . . . not. I'm in my own little bubble, not going anywhere at all."

"For me, it's traffic jams," he says. "You'd think after dealing with angry bulls, I could handle five o'clock traffic on the perimeter. But I'm the one letting everybody ahead of me and never moving forward myself." He laughs. "Oh, well. Never said I was the sharpest tool in the shed."

I laugh, too, and lean against him to say, *C'mon, of course you're the sharpest tool in the shed.* But I'm also thinking, *In all this realness, can't you let me know you recognize me? Please?*

I feel like I'm going crazy. I *am* going crazy, especially since I didn't exactly pull away after my shoulder nudge, and now he's slipping his arm around me in a manner that says, *Yes. You.* It's so very natural to turn and face him, my body gravitating toward his, and I say to my brain, *Oh, screw it.*

His kiss envelops me. His hand cups my neck, and his lips are warm against mine. He smells like fresh, clean soap.

Strength radiates from him, and it's so intoxicating, this extremely male energy of his, that it makes me aware of my own femaleness. I've never felt so *right* in my own body before. I am small and he is large, and I am soft and he is muscular, and these differences between us are good. They bring us together and make us whole.

There is a *whizz* and a *whistle* and a *boom*, and when Pete and I break apart, gold sparkles trail above us.

We watch, heads tilted to the sky. The fireworks dazzle my eyes and make my heart expand. Greens and golds and silver-spangled starbursts. Big boisterous flares interspersed with quieter *pfft-pfft-pfft*s that sprinkle down like popcorn.

The display goes on and on. Pete squeezes my hand through all of it, and I'm filled to bursting. The finale is a glorious release of light and color and sound, and from inside the club come jubilant cheers.

"Happy Fourth of July," Pete whispers. He pulls me toward him so that my back rests against his chest and his forearm hugs me close. His watch digs into me, and he rearranges when I shift. His wrist tilted toward him, he says, "Oh. Huh. Make that fifth." He kisses the top of my head.

I'm cozy and purring, and then his words soak in and I jerk upright. I twist his watch so I can read it: It's twelve twenty-five.

"Crap!" I say. I leap up. "I've got to go!"

"Wait!" Pete says as I sprint for the door. I hear him, but

the law of my childhood is permanently ingrained: "Thou shalt not break curfew." I'm already going to be late, which stokes my panic. I'm reacting without thinking.

The club is packed with bodies, and Porter Ann is nowhere in sight. I have to go, I have to go *now*, and after one last scan, I give up and hurry toward the front entrance. I'll text her from a cab, and tomorrow she'll call all giddy to catch me up on the stripper with the soulful eyes. I don't worry about leaving her with him, because she knows how to take care of herself. She'll switch to Perrier long before it's time to drive home, and if worse comes to worse, she knows how to call a cab.

I exit the club and stumble on the rough asphalt of the parking lot. A pebble drives into my bare foot, and I yelp.

"You okay, miss?" the bouncer asks.

Tears flood my eyes, and this time Porter Ann's not here to forbid them. They spill down my cheeks.

"I need a cab," I say.

He snaps his fingers, and a taxi pulls forward from the curb. As I climb in, something black and spiky sticks in my eye. I pull it free — it's an insanely long eyelash. I rub my eye, and more lashes, like spider's legs, come off on the back of my hand. Everything's falling apart.

"Where to?" the cabbie asks.

I take a shuddery breath and recite my address. But something's wrong inside me — well, a lot is wrong inside me — and as the cab pulls forward, it hits me what I'm doing. I'm running away — again. Which I promised myself I wouldn't do.

"Stop," I say.

"Whaddaya mean, stop?" the cabbie says. He isn't even out of the parking lot.

"I'm sorry, I'm so sorry," I say, hopping out of the cab. People might look at me funny, and Porter Ann will probably shake her head when I tell her, as if I'm an endlessly amusing kid. Mom will most certainly ground me.

But I don't care. I'm no longer going to stand still and let fear of other people's reactions hold me back. I'm going to think for myself, and I'm going to act on my thoughts. I'm going to find Pete and say loudly and clearly, "Here I am. Me. Megan. And I'm not letting you go again."

At the club's entrance, however, the bouncer refuses to let me through.

"Sweetie, c'mon," he says, jerking his chin at my feet. "You know I can't let you in like that."

"But . . . I was just here!" I say. "You saw me, you're the one who called the cab!"

He shrugs.

The front door flies open, and Pete rushes out. My sandals dangle from his hand.

"Megan," he says.

"You *do* know me!" I cry.

"You left so fast. . . . All this time, I've been hoping to run into you, ever since I first saw you . . ."

"You've been hoping to run into me? *Really?*"

"Well, yeah. That time, when it was just the two of us in the hall . . ." He blushes. "How could I not want to find you?"

I can't stop beaming. Ten seconds ago I was ready to dissolve in tears, and now my joy is a bluebird inside my chest.

"Beautiful, kids," the bouncer says. "One for the memory book." He lifts the red velvet rope. "Staying or going?"

Pete looks at me.

I want to stay, but it's not fair to leave Mom freaking. So I do the mature thing and tell him I have to go. "It's past my curfew," I say, making a face.

"Then I'll give you a ride home," he says.

"Okay," I say happily.

He drops to one knee, and I don't know what he's doing until he gently taps the heel of my foot. *Ohhh.* I place my hand on his shoulder as I slip one sandal on and then the other.

"Thanks," I say.

As we walk to the parking lot, he tells me he called the preschool and asked for my number, but the office lady wouldn't give it to him. He says he drove over in person, but couldn't work up the nerve to go in. He was afraid he'd be seen as a perv.

"You are *so* not a perv," I say.

"Thanks," he says. His mouth quirks up.

I have to kiss those lips, and so I do. I start to draw back, but he murmurs in protest and pulls me toward him again.

He gazes at me when we pull away. I can tell he likes what he sees. He leans forward and scuffs his thumb over my cheek.

"Here," he says, holding out one of the spider legs. "A wish."

"Oh, God," I say. "That's not even real. It's fake. It's an eyelash extension, can you believe it?"

*I* can't believe it — that I'm telling him this. But being with him makes all the falseness go away. And his mouth is quirking up again, because humans sure are funny.

"I say make a wish anyway," he says.

"I would . . . only I don't need to."

"Oh, yeah? And why's that?"

I slide up next to him. His arm slips around me.

"Because it's already come true."

★ ★ ★ ★ ★ ★ ★

# A NICE FLING IS
# HARD TO FIND

By Sarah Mlynowski

★ ★ ★ ★ ★ ★ ★

*Tuesday, July 10, 7:22 P.M.*

Dear TJ (aka Travel Journal),

I'm here! I'm on the plane! I did it!

I can't believe I'm actually going to FRANCE. I am so sophisticated.

Okay, fine, in my ratty sweatpants, T-shirt, and ponytail, I am not looking so sophisticated, but that's hardly the point. I AM GOING TO FRANCE. As soon as the plane takes off. In eight — wait, make that seven! — minutes.

I almost missed the plane due to my parents' fanatical hugging. My mom was full-on whimpering, and even my dad's eyes were glistening (although he tried to pretend he got dirt stuck in his contacts). I reminded them that I would only be gone for eleven days (one night on the plane, four nights in Paris, one night on a train, two nights in the Alps, and three nights in Nice — pronounced *Niece* — which is on the Riviera), but my mom would not calm down.

"Are you sure you want to go?" she asked, her voice shaking.

I nodded.

"But what if you break something?"

"Then I'll go to the hospital," I said, attempting to sound calm.

"But you don't speak French!"

"Mom, there's a translator with the tour."

"Well, then stay with the tour at all times," she ordered.

"Of course." Maybe.

"Don't talk to strangers, Lindsay," she warned.

"Sure." Please. The entire point of this trip is TO talk to strangers. Because in France, I will be wild. I will be wild and have a mad fling with a gorgeous Frenchman named Jacques or Jean-Claude who will look deep into my eyes and feed me Brie on bite-sized baguettes.

"Better safe than sorry," my mom said, and I rolled my eyes.

See, so far everything about my life has been careful. I've never been out of the US before. I've barely been out of New York State (one trip to Florida does not a world traveler make). I have a younger brother named Jack, a dog named Ralph, I live in a nice house on Long Island, I have a 3.8 GPA, my parents are happily married . . . and I've probably put you, dear TJ, to sleep. Because there is nothing remotely interesting, remotely scandalous, about my existence thus far. I never skip school. I never yell at my parents. I've never run for student council. Not that I'm dying to be class president or anything, but my point is that I never take any risks. My mom has always been ridiculously overprotective, especially since I'm a tad bit accident-prone. I wasn't allowed to do anything growing up — no gymnastics, no skating, no skiing. No fun. This trip is my chance to escape from my mother's overprotectiveness and live a little.

My chance to finally have a fling — with a hot foreign boy.

The snarky French flight attendant in her cleavage-revealing uniform is ordering me to put up my tray table for takeoff. We haven't even left yet, and I'm already causing trouble! Go me! ☺


*No-Clue-What-Time-It-Is-Since-We-Keep-Crossing-Time-Zones P.M.*

Dear TJ,

We're in the air! Wahoo! I think we're somewhere over the Atlantic. Perhaps over the Bahamas? Not that I can see the Bahamas. Looking out the window is like staring into a pool of black ink.

Becca is sitting next to me in the middle seat, paging through a *Teen Vogue*. Tommy, her twin brother, is on her other side, reading *Let's Go France*. About fifteen others from our teen tour are on this flight. Mike, one of our tour guides, who is sitting diagonally from us, is already balding, even though he can't be older than thirty. Joanna, the second tour guide, is sitting next to him. She's wearing tight jeans and a *Teens Tour France!* T-shirt. I'd peg her as around twenty-three, at least seven years older than we are. Her teeth are blindingly white, and she keeps turning back to us and smiling as though she's in school and this is her class photo. She has outrageously long fingernails painted bright pink. If she keeps those florescent fingers away from my foreign fling, we'll get along just fine.

Becca and I have already outlined our rules. We are very good about making rules. In third grade we had club rules, in the fifth we had Barbie rules, and in the sixth we introduced boy rules. Since we both had a crush on a scrawny boy named Chet, we decided we'd each have to choose someone else to like. No hurt feelings allowed. We never liked the same guy again. And I'd know, 'cause we tell each other everything. I'm the person she called when her parents separated. She fed me banana sorbet after I got my wisdom teeth pulled. She's going to be my BFF even when we're eighty and living on a beach in Florida, complaining about how our grandkids never call us and that we can't hear the TV.

"Here's my rule — I'm calling dibs on the Texan," she whispered soon after takeoff, motioning with her head to a guy in a *Teens Tour France!* T-shirt sitting four rows back, near the bathrooms.

"Oh sure, take the only cute guy on the trip," I said, poking her in the side.

"Uh, hello? Remember me?" Tommy asked, waving. "I am right here."

Whoops. "Sorry, Tommy," I said, laughing. "One of *two* cute guys on the trip." I felt bad about that one. Of course

Tommy's cute. Not in a hello-I-need-to-make-out-with-you kind of way, but in a isn't-he-sweet, brotherly kind of way. What can he expect? He looks too much like my almost-a-sister best friend for me to think of him any other way. They're not identical, but they both have dark brown hair and the same foreheads. Of course, he's almost six feet, and she's barely five foot four. And he has his dad's dark brown eyes, and she has her mother's hazel ones. And her lips are pencil-thin and his are full. When his are outlined in lip liner, they're especially humongous. *Why* would Tommy use lip liner? Part of one of our many "boomerang dares," which involved all of us having to do things we didn't want to do in the name of absurdity. In this case, we got to put makeup on him, but we had to drink Tommy's Tornado, which was string cheese, raisins, Tabasco sauce, and seltzer, in the blender. Yum. Not.

There's no mistaking me and Becca for twins. I have green eyes and light brown hair — stick-straight light brown hair. Boring, boring, boring. Maybe I should get highlights to liven up my look? Or not. Becca tried highlights last year, and they were tough to keep up. She also tried lowlights and pink-lights and extensions. . . . Becca likes to try a lot of things. I, on the other hand, have never tried anything different or exciting.

Until now.

I returned my focus to Becca. "You know what? You can have everyone on the tour," I said with determination. "I'm only considering men with accents."

"Go, you!" Becca exclaimed, putting her arm around me. "I raised you well, little one."

Becca likes to call me "little one" because, at five foot one, I am the only person she knows who is shorter than she is.

"Long Islanders have an accent," Tommy piped up with a grin.

"*Foreign* accents," I clarified. "Italians, Russians, Spaniards . . . but most especially, Frenchmen."

Tommy kicked off his Adidas sneakers and pushed them under the chair in front of him. "What about Brits? Or Australians? Who gets them?"

"Good question," Becca said. "I *do* like Brits. And Australian guys are super-sexy. They're all tanned, muscled, and blond."

"You can have anyone who speaks English," I told her. "The only language I'm speaking is the language of love."

That's when Tommy groaned and said, "You're such a cheeseball, Lindster." He reclined his seat, pulled out his iPod, and put in his earbuds.

Becca is poking my side now. She wants to play the travel Battleship she brought. Gotta go. Not that I'm GOING anywhere . . . except France . . . oh, whatever. Can you tell this is the first time I've ever kept a diary?


*Wednesday, July 11, 6:00 A.M. France Time!*
*Bonjour TJ!* We are here. *Nous sommes ici.* And by *ici*, I mean sitting on the cold floor of the baggage-claim area in Charles

de Gaulle International Airport, waiting for our backpacks to be spit out. Not that anything can get me down. Because I am in Paris — the land of romance.

When the plane finally landed, we followed Joanna through customs. Joanna began singing, *"Sur le pont d'Avignon, on y danse, on y danse!"* at the top of her lungs. No idea what she was saying, but I'm assuming it was in French. Everything was in French. The signs, the restaurants, the bookstores. Then we went through customs, where the man said, *"Bonjour,"* to me. *Bonjour!* How cute is that? I got an adorable stamp on my spanking-new passport, and then I snuck into *les toilettes* and now we're here in *le baggage* claim. Waiting. Oh there's mine, gotta go! Hmm, it looks insanely heavy. I think twenty T-shirts, fifteen pairs of shorts, and eight pairs of shoes may have been overkill.

Tommy is waving at me, trying to get my attention, possibly trying to let me know that my bag is coming around the bend.

Perhaps if I pretend not to see it he will pick it up for me?

He's doing it! He's doing it! Tee hee. What's French for gullible dork?

*A few hours later*
Even the trip from the airport to the hostel was exciting.

"Can you smell it?" I asked Becca as we stepped out of the airport doors.

"Smell what?" she asked, sliding on her oversized sunglasses.

"The fresh pastries! The hot coffee! The Chanel perfume!"

"I smell the diesel fuel," she said with a shrug.

Mike led us to our air-conditioned bus, and Becca and I moved to the back row and sat with our feet up. We cheered when we spotted the Eiffel Tower through the window. The driver sped along the highway like he had never heard the expression "speed limit," and I squeezed Becca's hand.

Now we are at the hostel, Les Quatre Saisons.

Which is ironic, considering this place looks *nothing* like the Four Seasons. Not that I've ever stayed at a Four Seasons, but I went to a wedding at one, and it looked nothing like this. And I bet the rooms were not dusty and packed with metal bunk beds.

Not that I'm complaining. I am not. I am very lucky to be in France. I had to beg, Beg, BEG my parents to let me come on this trip and do filing work at my mom's office for four months to help pay for it. The trip was Becca's idea to begin with. She wanted to just backpack across France, but my mother would have never gone for that. I'll admit it even freaked me out. So this was the best compromise. And since it wouldn't have been fair if Becca got to go to Europe without Tommy, here we *all* are. In Les Quatre Saisons. Stop number one.

There are six bunk beds in our room, which works out

because there are eleven of us: ten girls and one leader, Joanna. The guys are in a room down the hall. For the first time ever I am sleeping on the top bunk. (Sure, I can hear my mother's voice warning me that I might roll off and end up in a body cast, but I am ignoring her, thank you very much.) Becca is beneath me. Next to us are Penny and Penni (I am not making that up), best friends from a neighboring Long Island 'burb. This is how Penny introduced herself: "I'm Penny with a Y! This is my B-F-F Penni with an I!"

I'd mock her for using BFF in a sentence, but I think I just used it a few pages ago.

But it's not like I said it out loud.

Anyway, Penni with an I has blond hair and Penny with a Y is a brunette. They are wearing matching velour sweatsuits, rhinestoned flip-flops, and pigtails.

"I hate them," Becca whispered as she unrolled her sleeping bag.

Becca never shies away from making snap judgments. She never shies away — or is shy — about anything. Compared to her, Tommy is so quiet.

The other six girls on our trip are Britney, Rori-Ann, and Carrie from Jersey, who seem to be quite cliquey (they have not spoken a word to anyone but one another and have already taped photos of their boyfriends on the walls behind their pillows); Max and Kristin from Toronto (they have about five cameras between the two of them and have already snapped about seven hundred pictures); and Abby from Miami (who has the most ginormous breasts I have ever seen. She must be a thirty-six triple D). Abby has to share a bunk with Joanna. Our fearless leader seems to have recently ingested at least six cups of café, 'cause she is bouncing off the bunk beds. She has already unpacked her sleeping bag, changed into shorts and a tank top, unpacked all her clothes into neat piles on her shelf, and lined up her shoes.

Just watching her is exhausting.

So tired. Eyes heavy. Think I might just close them for a

*Still Wednesday, July 11, 9:15 A.M.*

Joanna let me sleep for about half a second before deciding that waking me up with a French song was the way to go.

*"Frère Jacques, Frère Jacques, dormez-vous? Dormez-vous?"*

Max and Kristin snapped pictures.

I changed into shorts, a fresh T-shirt, and running shoes ("Make sure you're wearing comfy sneakers!" Joanna chirped), located the bathroom down the hall, and washed up.

Now, the eleven of us are sitting on hard iron benches in a shaded garden behind the hostel, waiting for the boys to join us. What's taking them so long? I thought girls were the ones who took forever.

I hear some laughter in the distance. And now the side door is opening . . .

OH. MY. GOD.

\*　　\*　　\*

*Ten minutes later*

We're on one of those open-air buses going to the Eiffel Tower so I can't write, but I just want to say that I've found him! My fling! His name is Pierre and he is *gorgeous*. He is our French translator. He is eighteen, and he is tall and blond and has blue eyes the color of the cloudless Parisian sky.

MUST STOP WRITING CHEESINESS.

But he is hot.

He walked into the garden behind the hostel, followed by Mike, Tommy, and the other Teens Tour boys. Suddenly it was my turn to drool. Not that I was the only one. Oh, no, the other girls were all staring at the embodiment of French perfection with equal adoration.

"*Allo*," he said in an accent that made us all melt in our comfy sneakers.

"Hello," we responded. Max and Kristin snapped pictures.

"I am Pierre, ze French translator. I am very pleased to meeting you," he said, and smiled.

And we are even more pleased to meet you.

He went on to say that this was his second of four tours this summer, and that he hoped this would be the best of them all.

"Dibs," I whispered to Becca when I could find my voice.

"All right, you can have him," Becca said, turning back to her Texan.

Now I'm in the back row of the bus next to Becca, while Tommy and the Texan, whose name is Harold, oddly (what kind of a cowboy is named Harold?), are sitting in the row in front of us.

The boys want to know what I'm writing about.

None of your concern, American dweebs.

Pierre is sitting up front with Joanna and Mike. When we all introduced ourselves, he said allo and we had a full moment of eye contact when my heart nearly exploded. Bam! Of course since all the other girls were likely also feeling the bamming, I'll need to step up my game. Perhaps by not stopping to write in my diary all the time so I'll look less like an antisocial hermit and more like a friendly, outgoing international lady of fun.

*1 P.M.*

The sun is kissing my face, the wind is lightly blowing my hair, and I can't believe how lucky I am. I'm on the Eiffel Tower. ON THE EIFFEL TOWER! Cool, huh? And it looks just like it does at Epcot!

Yes, I'm aware that sounds dumb, and no, I didn't say it out loud.

But really. It looks exactly like its replica. Except it's ten times bigger. And it took us four hours to get up here since the line for the elevator was out of control. Next time I'll just climb it.

Anyway. The city is laid out before me like a French Monopoly board. Little cafés and bicycles and small boxy cars line the streets, and the air smells like warm bread. I could stay up here forever. From this height I'm not afraid of anything. Except falling.

*Thursday, July 12, way, way too early. Like 5:00 A.M.*
I am lying in my narrow bunk bed, which feels much higher than it did when I chose it, and I'm wide awake. Since Long Island is like six hours behind, I don't know why I'm up. But I'm glad to have a few minutes on my own, since yesterday was beyond busy. After the Eiffel Tower extravaganza, we hung out at this huge park called Champ de Mars and had a little picnic of baguettes and cheese (really!). Becca and I lay down on the grass and listened to the sounds of the city as we watched the small white clouds drift across the sky. Then we all went over to the Right Bank on the other side of town and were allowed the afternoon to explore. Becca wanted to go into all the fancy couture stores on Avenue Montaigne.

"Do we have to?" I asked. "The salespeople will know we can't afford anything."

"Then we'll have to look the part," Becca said, and pulled matching black scarves from her purse and tied them around our necks. Then she tied my hair into a twist and made me tuck in my shirt so I looked more presentable and instructed me to keep my sunglasses on at all times. She is too much.

Anyway, of course the stores were all glossy and polished but the salesladies smiled tightly and *Bonjour*ed us so I guess we had them fooled. Unfortunately the Pennies had the nerve to follow us and then the greater nerve to buy matching purses in the Louis Vuitton store. The two hundred Euros I have as spending money won't even cover a Vuitton purse *strap*. Not that I want a Louis Vuitton purse.

Later we all went to a café for dinner. Tonight we had mussels and fries. Of course I tried to sit next to Pierre, but it was like a mad dash to the table. Seriously. He took the head, while me, the two Pennies, Abby, and even Max and Kristin acted like we were playing musical chairs and the music had just been turned off, in an attempt to claim his neighboring sides. Abby and the Canadians went left but the Pennies and I went right and ended up in an unfortunate tangle for the seat.

I lost.

Booohooo.

I sat next to Becca instead. She intermittently talked to me between batting her eyelashes at Harold. Not that I blame her. He is definitely good for a summer fling, if you want to go the American route.

Which I don't. I am not going to waste my one trip away doing something ordinary. Anyway, you would not believe how sexy Pierre could make eating a French fry look. First he'd spear it with his fork, then he'd lift it off his plate, then he would slowly, oh so carefully, dip the fry into his mouth, and then gently bite the tip off with his teeth.

Tommy, on the other hand, who was sitting diagonal from me, kept stealing fries off my plate whenever I wasn't looking. Which was pretty often, considering I kept ogling Pierre. Tommy had his own plate of fries, so I don't know why he found it necessary and amusing to take mine.

Even though Pierre spent most of dinner laughing and talking to the ladies who had won the seat tug-of-war (Penny with a Y and ginormous-boobed Abby), he smiled at me twice. Yes, twice. Which I think is an excellent start, considering. Plus, halfway through the meal, he looked at me and asked, "Lindsay, did you like ze food?"

I did. But I like him even more. It's hot here in our room in the hostel. Too hot to sleep. I wish I had brought a thinner sleeping bag. I wish I had taken the bottom bunk.

I wonder if Pierre is still sleeping. What are the chances he's dreaming of me? Maybe I should sneak into the boys' room and spray my perfume on his pillow. Or, even better, maybe I should spray myself with said perfume. My hair is smelling a bit like eau de feet. Perhaps I should use this extra morning time to find the shower?

*An hour later — still really, really early*
I am back in my bunk bed. And I might need a shower from the shower. The water pressure was pitiful and the temperature

was beyond cold. It kind of felt like someone was holding ice cubes over my head and letting them slowly melt down my back. But I am refreshed! And now it is time to beautify so Pierre will see that I am fabulous and want to grab me in his French arms and kiss me passionately. Must find my guava-colored lip gloss in my makeup bag. It is my magic weapon. It brings out all the right coloring in my skin and makes my lips look luscious. I think it might be a kissing potion. It totally worked on Adam, my first — and last — boyfriend. We dated last year. I applied it before our first date and we didn't stop kissing for four months. Until I broke up with him. I was getting too attached to him and it was freaking me out. Better safe than sorry, right?

Okay, enough about the past. Time to get out of bed. Maybe I should wake up Joanna with a song. See how she likes it.

*Later today*

I am standing in Le Louvre. The most popular and amazing museum in the history of museums. It used to be a palace — and it definitely looks the part. Despite the packs of tourists, it is eerily quiet in here. People are speaking in hushed voices, like they're in a church. Everything is so gold and ornate.

At the moment, I'm desperately trying to get a look at the most famous painting of all time. Are you there, Mona? I can't tell. Because all I can see are other people's heads.

I've been standing here for ten minutes waiting for some space to clear up, but no go. Wait, wait, wait . . .

I just got a glimpse!

Honestly? She's not that attractive.


*Two hours later . . .*

Tommy and I are taking a break. We're supposed to be walking around for four hours, but it's a little cramped in there, and I kept getting accidentally pushed and stepped on and I started to feel a little claustrophobic and panicked that I would break something on the first real day. It's not like I break something once a week or anything, but I've broken enough bones to know that I'd like to try to stay in one piece if I can. I've broken two toes, my index finger, and my right leg (in separate stair, locker, gym-class, and bicycle-related incidents).

Anyway, Tommy wanted to check out the Louvre architecture from outside, and I said I'd go with him. Becca and Harold don't seem to mind admiring other tourists' heads. Or maybe they're admiring each other instead. . . .

I'm lying on the grass, getting some sun. Ah. The air here smells so French. Like a mixture of spice, grass, and cigarette smoke.

Tommy's around somewhere taking pictures. He has a fancy camera he bought at a garage sale on his street. Unlike all the other cameras on this trip, it's not digital. He brought two dozen rolls of film and plans on using the closet in his basement as a darkroom.

Now he's taking pictures of . . . me? No, something behind me. Pigeons?

I wish Pierre would come out here and say something to me in French.

*Friday, July 13, 8:00 A.M.*
Dear TJ,

We are on the bus, on our way to Versailles. I've got my own row today. Becca is sleeping in the seat across from me. She is sleeping because . . . she was up all night playing tongue hockey with Texan Harold! Of course she woke me up post-hookup to share all the glorious details. They were talking after dinner, and then she asked him if he wanted to go sit in the garden, and then she kissed him. They started fooling around right on the bench. And then they heard footsteps so they snuck into the women's *toilettes* (!!!!) and continued hooking up.

Okay, I'll admit it, I'm jealous. She is having a fling while I am not. Not for lack of trying. But I can barely get two seconds alone with Pierre. I sat next to him during breakfast, but he was absorbed in his *café au lait* and cigarette. The smoking thing is not such a turn-on, but maybe I could get him to quit. If only he would look at me.

I was wearing the guava and everything!

Perhaps I should start casting a larger fling net. Last night, from our window, I spotted a group of cute boy backpackers hanging out in the garden. I think they were Swiss or Austrian. Maybe I should make friends with them?


*11:00 P.M.*

Dear TJ,

Joanna is about to turn off the lights, and I'm beyond exhausted, but I want to tell you what happened today. Funny that I say you, as though you are a person and not simply me reading this when I get home, if ever. Although maybe you are my future daughter reading about my magical vacation in France! Hello, sweetie, I love you! Maybe I've married Pierre and he and I have had French-American love children!

Not. That is the whole point of a fling. A fling is a man you never see again. That's what makes it exciting. Harmless. Stringless. No one gets hurt if there are no strings attached, right? You kiss and maybe go to second and/or third base before saying good-bye forever. Perhaps you send perfumed wish-you-were-here postcards in the months that follow but that's as far as it goes.

Anyway, it's starting to occur to me that I may have no chance with Pierre. After our trip to Versailles (all green landscaped gardens, statues of angels, and a dizzying Hall of

Mirrors), we took a late afternoon/sunset cruise on the river Seine. Tommy was snapping artsy-type photos of the Paris skyline and the grand cathedral of Notre Dame, while Max and Kristin and the rest of the group were busy taking photos of the half-naked people on the quasi-beach. It's actually a man-made strip of sand on the banks of the Seine. And I say half-naked because some of the women were topless. And some of the men were wearing . . . G-string Speedos. Who knew they even made those?

The Pennies thought it was hilarious and kept pointing and ogling.

"What's the big deal?" Tommy asked, laughing, his camera dangling around his neck.

"Those girls are so immature," Becca said, wrinkling her forehead in disgust. Earlier today she had spotted them twirling their pigtails in Tommy's direction. Ever since then she had taken to eyeing them with suspicion.

"What's the big deal?" I asked. "He deserves a fling, too, no?"

"Those girls are *not* worthy of my brother."

Becca has some major big-sister issues. The fact that she's only four minutes older than Tommy doesn't faze her. When Janna Jacobs broke up with him last year, Becca accidentally-on-purpose spilled her Coke all over Janna's white linen capris. Tommy was not amused.

So I wasn't surprised when her next move on the boat was to call Tommy over to us and away from the Pennies.

After the cruise is when things got interesting. Becca and Harold went for "a walk," and Tommy and I regrouped in the hostel's courtyard, which is insanely pretty. It has three iron benches, small round tables, and moss growing between the cobblestones. Everything in Paris is so old and charming. I can picture what it was like to live here centuries ago.

Anyway, guess who was in the courtyard? The Swiss/Austrians. Except they aren't actually Swiss/Austrians, turns out they're Russians. Whoopsies. I would never have had the guts to talk to them on my own, but Tommy plunked himself down on the bench right beside them and began asking them all these questions. There were two of them: Vladimir and Mick. Vlad (that's what he told us to call him) is the hot one. He has blond hair and ridiculous cheekbones. If I had spotted him in a J.Crew ad, instead of in the courtyard of Les Quatre Saisons, I wouldn't have been surprised. Although J.Crew is pretty American. Maybe a Benetton ad? He and Mick were smoking clove cigarettes and laughing, and they told us about living in Moscow. And then Vlad showed me how to write my name in Russian: Диндсй. Or something like that. Apparently Ruskies have a totally different alphabet. Who knew?

An hour or so later, Becca and Harold joined us and the Russians said good night, but the way Vlad held my gaze for longer than necessary made me decide that he would be an attainable fling for me to focus on.

"Want to come with us to the Bastille Day parade tomorrow night?" I blurted out.

"Sure," Vlad said. "We'll meet you here. To pre-celebrate. At seven."

After we waved good-bye, Becca started jumping up and down on the bench. "Way to go!"

"Shush, they can still hear you," I said.

But whatever. I have a date! Kind of.

Joanna just turned off the lights. Can't see in the dark.

*A demain!*

*The afternoon of Saturday, July 14*

My boobs hurt. I am lying on my back, attempting to write in the air, because I cannot lie on my stomach.

Why, you might ask?

Oh, I'll get there. First off, Happy Bastille Day. That means it's France's Fourth of July.

But back to why my boobs are killing me.

Since we had a free day in honor of the holiday today, Becca and I decided we were going to hit the quasi-beach to get some sun. Pierre and Mike were taking the boys and some of the more athletic girls to play soccer.

We hiked down to the beach. It was kind of weird since it's in the middle of the city, but cool. We claimed our spot. We spread out our towels. I pulled off my shorts and T-shirt and then looked over at Becca.

Or shall I say, Becca's boobs. Oh, yeah, there she was, lying on her back, topless, for the world to see.

"What are you *doing*?" I shrieked.

She gave me a devilish smile. "What do you mean?"

"I can't talk to you when your *things* are on display." Not that she was out of place. Ninety percent of the women out there were topless. And it wasn't just the twenty-year-old locals. The tourists were topless. The GRANDMOTHERS were topless.

"Oh come on!" she said, laughing. "We're in France. We must!"

"Er, we?" I crossed my arms in front of my chest.

"Yes, we. Come on, Linds."

I was about to say no, but then I thought, well, why not? I wanted to be wild this trip, didn't I? I wanted to take risks and push myself out of my comfort zone.

And how much would this annoy my mom?

"Just whip it off!" Becca ordered.

Now or never. I had a brief moment of cold feet (or cold boobs), so here's what I did. I lay on my stomach, and then unclasped the back and slipped that sucker off. And then slowly turned around, my heart pounding. Then I squirted some suntan lotion in my palms, and did my best to smear it on my upper regions. But, come on, was I supposed to rub myself right there, like I was in *Girls Gone Wild*, Paris edition?

Becca started squealing and clapping, and there we were. Topless.

Honestly? It felt kind of cool. I mean it's not like my boobs have ever been allowed to see the sun before.

So I tanned. And closed my eyes. And pretended the Seine was the ocean. I was pretty relaxed about the whole thing until IT happened.

*"Allo, mes filles!"*

I opened one eye and then screamed.

Pierre. Back from soccer. Followed by a bunch of the other kids from the trip. Including Harold, Abby, and Tommy. The latter who was, thankfully, covering his eyes.

I rushed to flip over onto my stomach and immediately grabbed my shirt for cover. My cheeks, as well as other exposed parts of my body, were surely deep red.

I contemplated jumping onto one of the passing tour boats.

"Are you covered yet?" Tommy asked, hands still over his eyes.

"Yes," I squeaked.

"It's not you I'm worried about," he said, and I could see he was smiling. "It's my sister. Gross."

"Oh, shut up," Becca said, putting her top back on.

"All ze women are topless in France," Pierre said. "It's no good to be ashamed of your body." Pierre was definitely not ashamed. Like most of his countrymen, and unlike any of the American teen tour boys in their roomy swimming trunks, he was wearing a suit that was only slightly bigger than a Speedo.

For the record, I am NOT ashamed of my body. Or my boobs. I am perfectly happy with my boobs. But that doesn't mean I want my crush, my best friend's brother, AND my best friend's boyfriend to have free cable access to them.

"I'm happy with my body," Abby said in a singsong voice. She then untied the straps of her bikini top and tossed it to the ground.

Even I couldn't help but stare. They. Were. Huge. And perfectly tanned. Apparently this wasn't her first time setting them free in the sun.

Pierre's stubbled jaw dropped.

I might have to give up on Pierre and focus all my attention on Vlad. There is NO way I can compete.

Anyway, it's a good thing I put on my top when I did. Why? Because a few minutes longer might have given me first-degree burns. As soon as we returned to the hostel and I stepped into the shower and let the water (the low-pressure barely-there-water) dribble onto my left boob, I shrieked in agony. And then noticed that it was bright red. Lobster red. As in, worst sunburn of my life. Post shower of pain, I gingerly applied aloe vera.

Okay, now I have to get dressed for the parade. Yippee.

No, no, no. I will not let my sunburnt boobs get me down! I am in France! I will enjoy myself! I have plans with Vlad! There will be fireworks! Tonight is going to be the best night ever!

*Sunday morning, July 15, 2:00 A.M.*
OH. MY. GOD. This is a disaster. A GIGANTIC disaster. My life is ruined.

I don't even know where to start.

Okay, so we got dressed in our finest (almost finest — I was in too much agony to wear my adorable red strapless sundress, so had to settle for a loose black cotton shirt over cropped leggings instead). I put on the guava, and dragged Becca outside to meet the Russians.

"What if Vlad's sketchy?" Becca asked. "Is it really a good plan to hook up with him? You barely know him."

"You've only known *Harold* for a few days."

"That's different."

"Why?"

"He's American!"

Oh, please. "What is up with you? You're usually encouraging me to do crazy things."

"Am I?"

"Um, yeah. Have you seen the color of my boobs?"

Anyway, regardless of what Becca thought, the smile Vlad gave me when I stepped outside . . . well, it made me feel quite confident that he would be Mr. Fling. There would be some kissing action tonight, no doubt about it.

There would not, for obvious reasons, be second base action. My second bases were quite furious with me at the moment.

Tommy, freshly showered and sporting a pale brown buttondown shirt over jeans, was sitting beside Vlad, so I sat between them and said, "Hello boys."

And then I noticed the bottle of cheap champagne on the table.

"Cheers," Tommy said, and poured me a glass.

"Be careful," I told him, glancing around the garden. Alcohol was definitely not allowed on the trip.

"There is no drinking age in France," Vlad said in his cute Russian accent, as he took a gulp.

A second later, Joanna popped up and we all froze. "I see you," she said, covering her eyes. "But I'll pretend I don't. Since it's a holiday." She wiggled her index finger. "One glass and that's it."

I've never actually had champagne, but this seemed as good a time as any to try it. Since I'm in France. Where champagne comes from. I think. We all toasted and clinked and sipped.

Then Harold joined us, so we toasted and clinked and sipped some more.

I tried to focus on the plan — chatting up Vlad.

He told me he was backpacking across Europe for the

entire summer and that his next stop was Zurich. Then he was planning on going to Juan-les-Pins on the Riviera.

"You should come to Nice instead," I said, extra flirty. "We'll be there next week."

"Maybe I will," he said, inching closer to me. He smelled smoky and sexy.

"I heard the beach in Juan-les-Pins is much better," Tommy said, out of nowhere. "Do you know the beach in Nice is all rocks?"

Um, hello? We're trying to encourage him to join us, not convince him to stay away. I gave Tommy my best butt-out-annoying-boy glare, but he totally ignored me. Then he tried to convince Vlad to skip the Riviera all together and go straight to Spain.

Why, you wonder, was he talking crazy? Oh, you shall see.

Joanna returned with Pierre and Mike, and then the entire Teens Tour France! group, plus the two Russians headed down to the wide Champs Elysées for the parade.

Big mistake.

Why did I think it was a good idea to invite my potential fling out with the Pennies? They sidled up to him immediately and started yapping about who knows what. Pigtails, maybe? I wanted to claim him in some way, but what was I supposed to do, grab his hand? Put my arm around him? Pee on his shoe? That's what Ralph does to trees when he marks his territory.

I scouted the area to see where Pierre was, and as I suspected, he was in a conversation with Abby, who was bursting out of her bustier. Yes, it seemed that Vlad was my only hope.

The people in the streets cheered, the fireworks exploded into ribbons of red, white, and blue above the Eiffel Tower (who would have thought that France's flag used the same colors as ours?), but I couldn't concentrate. Instead, I watched the Pennies hog my fling.

"What is wrong with me?" I complained to Tommy. The two of us were standing together, squashed on the street between random celebrators wearing French flags. "I want to have a fling! Why aren't any men interested in flinging with me?"

"Lindster, I promise there are men interested in flinging with you. Maybe they just don't know that you're interested. Maybe they want to know they're not going to get shot down before trying anything."

"You are so right," I said, nodding emphatically. "I have to be more like your sister. Brave."

He cocked his head to the side and half-smiled. "Maybe it's not the fling that you're afraid of."

"Sorry?" I wasn't sure what he was talking about. My shoe got caught in a leftover streamer and I tried to scrape it off with my heel. The ground was such a mess. Bottles and gum and plastic cups.

He looked right at me and took a second to respond. "Why do you think you want to have a fling so badly?"

"What do you mean?" I said and tried to laugh. I looked

down at the ground and kicked one of the wine bottles. "Because it would be fun. Romantic. Adventurous."

"Is that the only reason?" he asked, and his forehead wrinkled. "Why are you only considering foreign guys? Why write off everyone on the trip? Why not try for something real?"

Now I didn't answer. I wasn't sure I liked where he was going with this.

"I think you're afraid of getting hurt," he said from right beside me. His voice was low, but I could still hear him.

I kicked another bottle. "Aren't you?"

And that's when —

Oh God, I can't even write it.

Deep breaths.

And that's when — Tommy tried to kiss me.

Oh, yeah.

And no, it wasn't the champagne playing tricks with my brain.

He stepped closer to me, then closer, and then I noticed that his face was moving toward mine.

At first I didn't realize what was happening. I thought one of the tourists had accidentally pushed him into me, and I shot out my arms to protect myself in case I fell. But then I realized that his eyes were closed (!) and that those full lips were not only pursed (!), but were coming straight at me.

So I ducked.

Unfortunately, since Tommy's eyes were closed, he didn't see that I was no longer there. So he kept moving his face forward. My not being there to receive said face threw him off balance, which caused him to trip over himself, and the next thing I knew he was splayed flat on his back in the middle of the Bastille Day parade.

Of course everyone in our group, as well as quite a few strangers, came rushing over.

And me? I was frozen. I was shocked.

My best friend's brother just tried to kiss me.

To KISS me.

What was that? Honestly I don't know what to make of it. I don't know, TJ, maybe YOU saw it coming. What with all his talk about why I wouldn't give someone on the trip a chance. But I thought he was being . . . theoretical. I mean, he, Becca, and I talk about this kind of stuff all the time. You know, fears and psychology and philosophy and life.

Anyway, Becca pushed passed me and helped her brother to his feet. "What happened?" she cried. "Did someone hit you?" She glared at the crowd, ready to beat up whoever had hurt him.

If only I could have disappeared into the crowd.

"I fell," he said, limping toward a sidewalk, and rubbing the back of his head.

And what was I supposed to say? What was I supposed to

do? Why would Tommy try to kiss me? He's never shown any type of interest in me. Why tonight? Did he think I came on to him? Did he think I wanted him to be my fling?

I can't hook up with Tommy!

Yes, he's cute and a nice guy. But it cannot happen. For many, many reasons.

1.  I am not attracted to him! At least, I don't think I am.
2.  He's my best friend's brother. My best friend's TWIN brother. You can't hook up with your best friend's twin brother for many obvious reasons. One being, your best friend will never speak to you again once you and said twin break up. That's what people in their teens do — they break up. It's not likely that two sixteen-year-olds will get married. I'm not saying it's impossible, but a smart gambler would wager that it's highly unlikely. So, either I break up with him, or he breaks up with me. If I break up with him, Becca hates me for hurting her brother. If he breaks up with me, then I hate him for breaking up with me, and then I spend the next ten years avoiding him, and then what do I do when Becca wants me to be the maid of honor at her wedding?

    Or what if us hooking up doesn't even lead to a relationship? What if it's the sloppiest, most disgusting kiss in the history of kissing? What if he bites my tongue by mistake and gives me a lisp? It would always be awkward between us. I would never be able to hang out at their place watching TV or making English muffin pizzas in the microwave.

3. Tommy is not foreign. My fling is supposed to be someone I will never see again. Not someone from my own city, from my own high school, or especially someone I have known since nursery school.

After the encounter, I could not, would not, look at Tommy. And he could not, would not, look at me.

I could barely summon the appropriate concentration to flirt with Vlad. Or Pierre. In fact, I totally lost Vlad in the crowd and didn't even get a chance to say good night to him after the parade. Who knows if I'll ever see him again? Sure, he's staying in the hostel, but I don't want to be a fling stalker.

Tommy has ruined everything. What was he thinking? Was he drunk? Suffering from heatstroke? Perhaps my guava is even more powerful than I've realized?

And the worst part is that I can't complain to Becca. *Hey, your brother hit on me, our friendship is awkward from this morning forward, and happy Bastille Day to you.*

Everyone is fast asleep. Well, not everyone. Penny with a Y is missing. Her sleeping bag is still zipped tight. Where is she?

Is she hooking up with my Vlad?

She so is.

Who does she think she is, hooking up with some random guy? Slut.

Now I'm in an even worse mood. Maybe I'll go to sleep and wake up back in Long Island.

*Still Sunday, still in France, 7:00 A.M.*
No luck. I'm still here.

Joanna just woke me up with *"Les Poissons, Les Poissons, hee hee hee hon hon hon."* Oh yes, she broke out *The Little Mermaid*.

TJ, would you mind very much if I used you to hit Joanna over the head?

*10:00 P.M.*
We're on the train, headed toward the Alps. I wish I was under the train.

It's not the train per se that's bad. I don't mind the train. I actually like the train, usually. You can sit and do nothing but lazily watch the scenery roll by the window. In this case, scenery of the green French countryside. Except I am too cranky to be lazy, and it's too dark out to see the fields of sunflowers or whatever.

After the early wake-up call, we went to Notre Dame. I think I would have appreciated the gargoyles and towers more if I'd been in a better mood. Unfortunately I couldn't even hide behind a camera, since I can't find mine. Of course Tommy was snapping away, looking all professional about it.

Tommy, who I still haven't spoken to.

Anyway, it took us at least an hour to get up Notre Dame, but from the top you could see 360 degrees around Paris. But then we had to climb down, and I almost passed out on the stairs, because they were the swirly kind and I felt a moment of panic that I would slip, fall, and have to be put in a body cast. Becca kept saying don't look down, but how can you not? I got nauseous, and had to sit down for a few minutes, which the people behind me in line did not appreciate.

I'm not sure exactly how I got down — all I remember is that Becca was holding my hand.

Then we went back to the hostel and packed up and checked out.

Of course I kept an eye out for Vlad, but did I see him? No. Potential fling number two slipped right through my fingers. Good thing potential fling number one is stuck with us. Good-bye, Vlad, good-bye. Love always, Диндсй.

"We'll always have Paris," Becca said as we strapped on our gigantic backpacks. The trick is to sit down on the floor, put your arms in, and then hoist yourself into a standing position.

At the train station, Joanna purchased us all overnight tickets to the French Alps. Each car on the train has two bunk beds and fits four. Since Joanna said we could pick our own cars, it should have been Harold, Becca, me, and Tommy. But, when it came time to get into our cars, Tommy was conspicuously absent. It was so obvious. To me anyway. Fortunately, Tommy hadn't said anything to Becca and Harold about what happened, so they didn't understand where he was.

"What if he's not on the train?" Becca asked, concerned.

"I'm sure he's here somewhere," I muttered.

"I don't think so. I'm going to look for him," she said.

So then it was Harold and me in the car.

"Hey."

"Howdy."

Oh, the conversation was wild.

I could hear Becca stomping about, checking the other cars with a, "*Excusez-moi, excusez-moi.*" Until I heard, "Oh. There you are. Why didn't you sit with us? I thought we'd left you in Paris."

"Oh, hey. I'm going to stay here." Tommy's voice was low and rumbly.

"Why?"

I couldn't hear the answer, but then Becca returned to our cabin and closed the door. She climbed into the bottom bed next to Harold. "That was weird."

La, la, la.

She draped her legs across Harold's thighs. "I'm going to have a long talk with my brother. He better not be making moves on one of the Pennies. They are so lame."

And then to make the night even more excruciating, that's when our door slid open. "Excellent," Joanna said. "You have an extra bed. I'm going to join you."

I wasn't the only one unhappy about this development. Harold had to move to the bunk above Becca, since sharing a car was one thing but sharing a bed was another.

Then half a second later, Pierre popped his sexy head into the car, looked around and said, "Oh, zis room is full. *Tant pis.*"

Javelin through the heart. Pierre separated from Abby for the first time all week and my car is full.

Finally the train took off . . . and here's my question: How am I supposed to sleep on a moving bed?

*Monday, July 16, 6:45 A.M.*
I just ran into Tommy outside the bathroom.

After tossing and turning and repeatedly banging the back of my head against the train wall, I finally fell asleep. Or was knocked unconscious. Whatever. But then I woke up, finding that I had somehow rolled off my bed onto the floor. Good thing I had a bottom bunk. I decided to try and locate the bathroom.

When I came out, I found Tommy waiting by the door.

"Hey," I squeaked, looking at the ground.

"Oh, hi."

Pause. Silence. Neither of us moved.

"Listen, Lindsay?"

"Yes?"

"I'm — I'm sorry about what happened."

"No biggie," I said quickly.

"It's just —"

I had to stop him from continuing. It suddenly occurred to me that he could actually like me. And once he put that out there, well, there was no going back. "It was the bubbly, right?" I added in a rush.

"Oh . . . yeah. The champagne."

"Goes straight to the head. Don't worry," I reassured him. "I won't say anything to Becca."

He looked out the window, at the trees in the darkness. "Sure."

"We friends?"

"Of course. Friends." He turned back to me and smiled.

Then we both stood there. And then he took a step toward me. . . .

Oh, no not again, I thought. So I jumped back. "Tommy, we talked about this."

He looked confused for a second, and then he laughed. "I was just going to the bathroom."

Right.

So now I'm the girl who thinks my best friend's brother is constantly trying to jump her. Awesome.

I returned to my bed and tried to fall back asleep, but to no avail.

Now Harold and Becca are awake and giggling — Harold must have climbed into Becca's bed during the night, because they're all curled up together like two puppies.

Joanna is still sleeping. Which is why I take great pleasure in opening the blinds.

Ha!

The view of the sun rising over the mountains is quite spectacular. I would take a photo if I could find my camera. Maybe today will be a good day. We're going white-water rafting. I have never been white-water rafting. That is not something my mother would ever agree to let me do. In fact, she explicitly told me after seeing it on the itinerary that I had to sit it out.

Tough.

I am going to do it. I am not a child. I can be careful.

It is pretty cool that I'm white-water rafting in the French Alps.

What did you do today? Oh, I went white-water rafting in the French Alps. You?

Beats going to the mall.

*Still Monday, 5:00 P.M.*
I'm in the hospital.

Nice, huh?

Don't worry, it's nothing major.

Really.

Let me start at the beginning.

When we arrived, we checked into our chalet, which was much nicer than the hostel in Paris. We're four per room, each room holding just two bunk beds. Somehow Becca and I got stuck with the Pennies. The good news is that each room has its own small bathroom. I mean, really small. The shower is — I'm not kidding — on top of the toilet. I made Becca take a picture.

Anyway, we put our stuff away, ate croissants and cheese (the amount of cheese in this country is out of control. I've only been here a few days and I've already ingested more than my body weight. If I'm not careful I'm going to develop a lactose intolerance), put on our bathing suits, and got picked up by the white-water-rafting shuttle buses.

Before we were placed onto said rapids, we divided ourselves into small groups. Ours was Harold, the Pennies, Becca, Tommy, Pierre (!!!), the rafting guide, and me. I don't know how I got so lucky, but Pierre and Abby were clearly having some sort of lovers' quarrel because Abby kept glaring our way. Anyway, we were all fitted with red helmets and yellow life jackets and handed paddles. I tightened my equipment, scooted over to the edge, made my knuckles turn white from gripping my paddle — and practically had a heart attack when a glistening Pierre took the spot beside me.

The little hairs on his calves were fully touching my (hairless) legs. "Ready?" he asked.

Terrified.

I took a deep breath of the fresh mountain air and tried to calm myself. Then I tried to imprint the stunning scenery in my brain. How could anything bad happen here? The mountains were lush and green and capped with white. Besides, if rafting was actually dangerous, they wouldn't let unsuspecting tourists do it, would they? Especially Americans. Hello. We sue.

Finally we began rafting. Basically you paddle down the river until you hit the rapids, then you hold on for dear life. The first set of rapids weren't bad. They were a class two. We paddled, we stopped paddling, we held on, the water splashed in our faces . . . but we all made it.

The second one was a class four. Since one of the other boats was only a minute ahead of us, we could see them in the distance. They went over the rapids and — BAM! Rori-Ann and Britney almost went over the side. Max and Kristin took pictures.

And then it was our turn. We paddled and paddled and held on, held on to the yellow rope, and then we were zooming —

The next thing I knew, I was flying headfirst out of the boat and into the rocky water.

My life flashed before my eyes. My dog, Becca, my mother. My mother who was going to kill me if the rocks didn't. Tommy.

Tommy?

Once I hit the subzero water and realized that I was still alive, I caught my breath and spotted the panicked look on Becca's face. Then I saw that Tommy was hanging out of the raft, trying to grab on to me. The guide was yelling at him in both French and English to sit down, and motioning for me to swim to a shallower area.

"I'm okay!" I sang out. And I was. Cold, but fine.

But is my fall responsible for my hospital visit?

Nope.

The guide hoisted me back into the raft.

"Are you all right?" Becca and Tommy asked simultaneously.

I nodded yes, teeth chattering.

"Did zat hurt?" Pierre asked, quickly warming me up by wrapping his arms around me.

"A little," I said, hoping he would not move his arms. EVER.

"You're shivering," he said, rubbing my shoulders.

"Cold in there."

"Yes, but we will be *chaud* in ze hot springs next."

"Right," I said. That was the next stop for today. I didn't know exactly what hot springs are, but I was guessing they were like some sort of natural hot tub. Hot-tubbing with Pierre? Sounded good to me.

When we were done, we unsnapped our jackets, took off our helmets, picked up our paddles, and walked back to the boathouse. Becca was beside me, red-cheeked and laughing, when she clucked her tongue. "Penny with a Y hooked up with my brother on Bastille Day, and on the train. How gross is that?"

And that's when the paddle slipped out of my hand, landed on my foot, and sent me to the hospital.

When it first landed, I howled in pain.

Joanna ran over.

"I'll be fine," I told her. "This happens all the time."

She crouched in front of me. "I think we need to go to the hospital," she said.

"No!" I whined. "It's my middle toe. There's nothing they can do. Trust me, I've broken it twice already."

"Maybe," Joanna said. "But we're legally responsible to get it checked out. I can't have your parents suing me."

"They won't! I promise!" If they'll blame anyone, it'll be me. "I'm sure I'll feel much better once I soak my foot in the hot springs."

"No way," Joanna said, shaking her head. "You guys go on ahead to the springs. We'll see you back at the lodge."

The shuttle bus dropped us off. Us being me and Joanna.

No hot springs for me. And no Pierre, either. I convinced him that the rest of the group would need his translation skills more than I would. This was humiliating enough without him being there.

So now Joanna and I are sitting on plastic chairs in the

waiting room. My foot is shoeless and resting on the seat beside me. Two of my toes are bright blue. It's not pretty.

"Poor you," she says.

*"C'est la vie,"* I say with a sigh.

*Four hours later*

My foot isn't broken — but one of my middle toes is. And just like I said, there's nothing they can do for it either, except wrap it to the big one and hope for the best.

I missed the hot springs. I missed dinner too. When I got back to the lodge (hungry, extra-cranky, and in pain), I unlocked my door and walked in on Becca and Harold making out.

I slammed the door.

"Sorry, hold on one sec!" Becca yelled.

I waited. And waited. And hobbled.

Finally she allowed me into my own room.

Becca and Harold just went for a walk, and now I'm sitting up in my bed grumbling. Becca is making out with Harold, and the Pennies are missing, so Penny could very well be making out with Tommy. I can't believe they're an item. How could he try to kiss me, and then hook up with *her* right afterward? See, that's why relationships are scary. A guy says he likes you and them, BAM! He likes someone else.

And Pierre . . . well Abby spent the entire evening with Pierre, showcasing her fabulous body in the hot springs. If reality TV has taught me anything, it's that they are right now rolling around together as I write.

Everyone has someone.

And what do I have? A broken middle toe and burnt boobs.

*Tuesday, July 17, 3:30 P.M.*

It's drizzly and cold. I'm sitting at a café, drinking *café au lait*, miserable. This trip sucks. France is evil.

"Today we're going on a hike!" Joanna exclaimed this morning.

I cannot go on a hike. Those with incapacitated toes barely walk, never mind climb the Alps. Becca offered to stay and hang out with me, but I insisted she go. She loves to hike, and I didn't want to suck her into my personal web of misery.

So I hobbled over to a nearby boutique. I saw a pretty purple dress in the window. I asked the salesgirl if I could try it on. She said *oui*. It didn't fit.

She then yelled, "*Zut alors!* You waste my time! Why you are waste my time?"

I hobbled out.

Now I am alone. Sitting at a café. Eating a croissant and brie.

Tomorrow we leave for Nice, the last leg of our trip. I can't wait for this to be over. I want to go home. To my house. To my family. To my dog.

The waiter who keeps bringing me cheese is kind of cute. Kind of. Not really. But kind of.

Maybe I should grab him by the collar, plant a wet one on his lips, and that would be that.

I'll guava-fie and smile pretty and see what happens.


*Two minutes later*

My guava is missing. I emptied my entire purse on the table and I do not see it. It must be in my backpack. It must.


*5:00 P.M.*

It's not. It's gone.

I must have left it on the train. Or in the Alps. Or in Paris. It's probably partying it up with my camera.

I have looked everywhere. I wish Becca were here to help me, but she's too busy traipsing through the mountains with Harold.

AHHHHHHHHHHHHHHH! France has not only stolen my camera, my walking capability, my potential flings, and my happiness, but it has now stolen my guava!


*Wednesday, July 18, 12:30 A.M.*

I have good news and I have bad news.

First the good.

We were in the restaurant of the chalet, about to have *steak frites*. We were sitting at a long rectangular table. I sat next to

Becca at one end. Abby was sitting at the other. The seat next to her was empty. The seat next to me was empty. Pierre walked in.

Who did he chose? Me. He chose me. He sat down right next to me. Ha! Go me! And to think that last night I was ready to write off the entire trip. Yet here I am back in the game, even without my guava.

"Hi, Pierre," I said. "How are you?"

"I'm sorry," he said, smiling. "I don't understand you. Can you ask me how I am in French?" That is what Pierre is supposed to do, after all — encourage us to speak French.

I picked up my fork and twirled it in my fingers like a baton. "I don't know how to speak French."

He leaned in closer to me. I could smell the cologne on his neck. "Repeat after me. *Bonjour, Pierre. Comment ça va?*"

"*Bonjour, Pierre,*" I parroted. "*Comment ça va?*"

"*Bien. Et toi?*" he said.

"*Bien. Et toi?*" I repeated.

"No, now you have to answer me. I said, 'Good and you?' And now you must tell me how you are."

"I'm good. Thank you, Pierre. I'm starving and looking forward to dinner. What do you recommend I order? How do I say that?"

"*Ça va bien,*" he said, sounding extra accenty and sexy. He was rolling his R's and everything. "*Merci, Pierre. J'ai faim, et je veux manger. Queseque tu recommandes manger?*" Then he added with a laugh, "*Comment je dis cela?*"

"That was *way* too much to repeat," I said.

He gave me a big knee-weakening smile. "You must try."

So he spent the rest of *le dîner* teaching me *le French*. Did you know that plate is *plat*? That fork is *fourchette*? That glass is *verre*? How smart am I? I can now name my entire place setting in French and spell my name in Russian.

If any of my teachers in school had been this sexy, I'd be multilingual.

Anyway, there I was enjoying my educational dinner when Tommy and Penny with a Y had to come and annoy the heck out of me. First of all, they walked into dinner TOGETHER, and his cheeks were all flushed and she was all giggling, and then he held out her chair for her. Puke. But that's not what really bugged me. It's when I saw it.

Her lips.

They were glossy. They were orangey. They'd been . . . guava-fied. Oh, yes. I am 99.9999% sure that Penny with a Y stole my guava. Not that I can accuse her. Yet.

I spent the rest of dinner trying not to stare.

First she steals Tommy, and then she steals my lip gloss? Did she take my camera, too?

*12:32 A.M.*

Not that I think Penny stole Tommy.

*12:45 A.M.*

Because he wasn't mine. He was my friend, sure, but he didn't belong to me. One thwarted kiss does not a boyfriend make. I don't even like Tommy! I mean, I like him as a friend, but that's it. I am not looking for or wanting another boyfriend.

*1:15 A.M.*

Obviously I'm going to have to search Penny's stuff right now while everyone is asleep.

*2:10 A.M.*

Well, that didn't work out as planned.

I shimmied down the bunk bed and then snuck over to her backpack. Which was unlocked. And which was also red and covered in designer labels. Instead of flags, Penny with a Y decided to sew I ♥ Juicy patches onto her bag. She's a citizen of Bloomies.

I got down on my hands and knees, unzipped it, and began feeling my way through her clothes.

"Lindsay, what are you doing?"

I froze. Penni with an I was awake and even in the dark I would see her glaring at me.

"I'm uh . . . looking for a tank top. It's so hot."

"But that's not your bag."

"What?" I feigned confusion. "Whoops! It's so dark in here I can't see anything."

"Why would yours be under our bunk bed?"

Excellent question. "I thought I put it there."

I don't know why I was making excuses to her, when it was her friend who (99.9999% sure) stole my stuff.

Once I removed my hands from inside her friend's bag, took out a tank top from my own (kind of had to), and returned to my sleeping bag, Penni reluctantly stopped glaring at me. Although first she double-checked both her and the other Penny's bag and locked them both.

And here I am. Writing. With my flashlight. Again.

In case you're wondering — my toe still hurts. And so do my boobs.

*5:30 P.M.*

Nice is not that nice.

We arrived by train this afternoon. We once again had to divide into rooms of four, but this time the Pennies arranged to stay with Max and Kristin. Wonder why. Anyway, Becca and I bunked with Abby and Joanna. We quickly changed into our bathing suits and met the rest of our group on the "so-called" beach. I write "so-called" because there is no sand. Only rock. Okay, fine, it's still pretty gorgeous. The coastline goes on forever and the water is bright emerald. Large, glamorous hotels line the beach and boardwalk. We hung out on a public beach, but just to the left of us was a private club area complete with white beach chairs, fluffy plum-colored towels, and bar service.

Because of the rocks, some of the guys had already bought foam mats to put their towels on, so we followed their lead and bought our own from a little shop on the boardwalk.

Then I set myself up — and declined to remove my bikini top, thank you very much. Becca kept hers on, as well.

But Abby and the Pennies? They were on full display.

I enjoyed the sun for an hour, but then felt my skin sizzling and thought I should take a little stroll, broken toe be damned. I hobbled down the beach, passing cafés and bars and beach clubs and sun umbrellas and yapping dogs, until I reached a path that took me uphill. I walked until I reached the cobblestones of old Nice and a railing that showcased the most incredible view of the beach I have ever seen. And now I'm sitting here, taking it in.

Breathing. Seeing. Riviera-ing. Actually, Nice is nice after all.

You know what I just realized? I have three nights left on this trip, and I am not going to spend them being miserable.

So what if I have no camera? I have you, TJ. You'll always remind me of my trip.

And so what if I have no fling? I have . . . well, I doubt you're a good kisser.

*Thursday, July 19, 3:00 P.M.*

See? It works. As soon as you make peace with yourself, good things happen. You'll never guess who I saw on the beach. . . .

I had set up my foam mat next to Becca's and closed my eyes when I felt someone blocking my sun.

Vlad! Looking hot and Slavic. "Hello," he said. "I have been searching for you."

He! Was! Looking! For! Me! I quickly sat up. "Hi, Vlad," I purred. "How was Switzerland?"

He sat down at the foot of my mat and told me all about Zurich. They had arrived in Nice two nights earlier and had been looking for us.

"Want to swim?" he asked.

"Sure, but I'll need some help," I said, motioning to my foot. He took my hand (took my hand!) and led me down to the water.

Now the beach may be covered in pebbles, but the ocean is as gorgeous up close as I thought it would be. And it feels almost as warm as bathwater. Azure blue, sparkling bathwater. Almost as stunning as Vlad's green eyes . . .

Sigh.

"Will you meet me tonight?" he asked. "It is my last night here. Tomorrow we go to Spain."

"Yes! I have to go to dinner in the old city with my tour group, but I can meet you as soon as I'm done."

"Perfect. You will meet me at Whiskey Disco? At 10? We will dance?"

Hooray! Of course I agreed. Dancing with Vlad! Kissing Vlad on the dance floor? Hello, *fling*! "Why don't you stay two more nights? And then go to Spain on Sunday?" I offered.

He shook his head. "That is not plan."

Okay then. Must stick to plan.

"Don't forget," he said, putting his hand to his shirtless, now wet chest. "Tonight."

Forget? How could I?

Now that you're all filled in, I gotta go shower and look extra fabulous.


*9:50 P.M.*

Oh my. I need to think. Think, think, think. I am sitting on a lounge chair in the Marriott's private beach area trying to clear my head.

I have big news. BIG NEWS.

Pierre came on to me.

Yes! Finally! Really! We all walked over as a group to the old city. The cobblestoned roads were so old and quaint, and the streetlights flickered like candles, and the entire area smelled like the garlic and warm pasta and wine emanating from a nearby restaurant.

We sat down at yet another long table. Pierre sat beside

me. Becca and Harold sat on my other side. Tommy and Penny sat across from them.

Abby, at the other end, glared. I looked at my watch.

We ordered. Pierre had a glass of merlot.

Tommy started talking in a French accent. Penny kept giggling.

We ate fries and mussels. Abby continued to glare. Penny continued to giggle.

Pierre had another glass of wine.

I looked at my watch again.

Pierre, very gently, put his hand on my thigh.

No one else could see, because his hand was under the table. He leaned toward my ear and whispered, "Lindsay, *comment ça va*?"

Clearly, this wasn't another French lesson.

"Um, *bien. Merci*." Had I just thanked him for touching my thigh? I think so, because he then started to caress said thigh.

"After dinner, you want to promenade on ze beach? I have a *merveilleuse* spot to show you." Still caressing. "It is romantic. Just we *deux*?"

Just the two of us? Tonight? Of all nights? "But I —"

He put his finger to his lips, and then said, "We will meet at ten. We will practice your French." He winked and then removed his hand from my leg and returned to conversing with the rest of the table.

When it rains, it rains buckets of men.

My heart was pounding hard and I glanced around to see if anyone had witnessed the conversation . . . and caught Tommy's eye. His expression was — well, it wasn't nice. His nose and forehead were wrinkled and his lips were pursed like he'd just eaten something disgusting. A bad *moule*? He shook his head and turned away.

What is HIS problem? HE'S hooking up with some random person. Why shouldn't I?

After dinner, I walked to the beach to regroup. Not only could I not physically meet both Vlad and Pierre, but I wanted ONE fling. Not two! Not two on the same night! That was just . . . dirty.

Now what am I supposed to do? I have plans with two different flings at 10 P.M.! But who should I chose? Who do I like better?

Vlad is a sexy Russian. He looks like a supermodel.

Pierre is a sexy Frenchman. He may or may not have already hooked up with someone else on the trip.

Who is a better fling?

Here's what I need to do. Visualize kissing both of them and see which one I prefer.

I'll start with Vlad.

Yes, I can see that . . . kind of . . . I mean . . . I'm not getting excited by the idea or anything. I don't know anything about him. Nothing. Just that he's Russian, smokes clove cigarettes, and likes to travel.

Hmm. Interesting. Pierre? He's a charmer. Good teacher. Kind of sweet.

I imagine my lips touching Pierre's . . . and . . . nothing.

Both of them — it's like imagining kissing my sleeping bag. What is up with that? I have to want to kiss someone. Okay, I'm going to close my eyes and whoever's lips I see are going to be the lips of my fling.

Oh. No.

I just saw the lips of . . . Tommy?

*Friday, July 20, 12:30 A.M.*

It's late. And I'm in my room. Alone. Kicking myself. Or rather, kicking my sagging mattress. SLAM.

I didn't meet Pierre. And I didn't meet Vlad. After Tommy's lips popped into my head, I couldn't stop thinking about how sweet Tommy is, and about the look on his face when I'd ducked during the parade in Paris.

My second big epiphany of the trip was this:

I like Tommy.

Really like him. Did I always like him? Probably not. But just because I never thought of him that way doesn't mean he couldn't BE that way. Maybe the idea just needed time to seep in. Like suntan lotion.

So, of course I couldn't hook up with Pierre or Vlad. Not now, when I know I have real feelings for Tommy.

Which is a bit of a problem. Considering that Tommy

barely talks to me anymore. And the look he gave me tonight — it was pretty much open disgust. He hates me. And on top of that, he's obviously into Penny. And on top of that, he's still Becca's twin brother! So even if he forgives me and stops liking Penny, I still can't go for him. See how messed up my life is?

I hate France. I hate everything French. I hate French songs, I hate French fries. And most especially I hate French kissing. Not that it matters because in all likelihood I will never do it again.

Oh, crap, now I'm crying and I hear a key in the door —

*1:10 A.M.*

I'm sitting in the lobby, on the ratty purple couch.

Why?

Becca and Harold caught me crying my eyes out. "What's wrong?" Becca asked, running over to me.

"E-e-everything," I blubbered.

"Harold, I'm sorry, I have to talk to Lindsay," she said to him. "We'll hang out tomorrow."

"But we only have two more nights together!" he cried.

"But she's my best friend," she said, giving him a quick kiss on the lips. "Tomorrow." Then she climbed up to my bunk bed. "What happened?"

By this time I was practically hyperventilating. How could I tell her?

"You have to tell me," she said.

"I can't!" I wailed. What was I supposed to say? *I think I have the hots for your brother?* I couldn't. I just couldn't.

She placed both her hands on my shoulders. "Is it about Tommy?"

KABAM! "How did you know?" I gasped, eyeing her warily.

"How did I know that Tommy was in love with you? Are you kidding me? I've known since third grade."

DOUBLE KABAM! "What?"

Then she laughed. "He's always had a thing for you, Lindsay. Why do you think he insisted on coming on this trip?"

Whaaaaaaaat? "Why did you never tell me?"

"Because I didn't want to weird you out," she said matter-of-factly. "I knew you didn't like him that way and I didn't want you to feel uncomfortable." Becca rolled her eyes. "But then he had to try and kiss you on Bastille Day —"

At this point I nearly fell off the bed. "You *knew* about that?"

She nodded. "Never mind knew — I *saw*. I would have beaten him up, but he did a solid job of beating himself up. He felt awful. He hadn't been planning it or anything, but then he thought that maybe you felt the same way. . . ."

"But I —"

"I know you didn't. He's my brother and I love him to

death, but you're my best friend and I love you too. I want both you guys to be happy. I hated that you two were suddenly all awkward around each other. That's why I lied and told you he was hooking up with Penny with a Y. So you wouldn't feel weird. I know how you get about these things."

I did a double take. "Wait a sec. Are you telling me that he *isn't* hooking up with Penny?"

"No. Never. For some reason he thinks she's sweet, but he's not interested in her. He only has eyes for you."

"But she was out all night! Who was she with?"

"Who knows. Vlad? Or Pierre possibly. Harold said he's a major player. He hooks up with all the girls on his teen tours. The rumor is that he's already made out with Abby, Max, and even Kristin."

Vile.

"But, anyway," she continued, "don't worry about my brother. His feelings are obviously upsetting you, so I'll talk to him again. I saw that he was giving you his googly eyes again at dinner, and he'll have to stop that. I don't want you creeped out. When we get back home, everything will go back to normal, we can all try and forget any of this ever happened and then —"

"But I don't want to forget," I blurted out.

She paused. "You don't?"

"I think I'm in love with your brother," I whispered.

Now it was Becca's turn to almost fall off the bed. Except,

she did fall off the bed. She did a weird sommersaulty backward thing and landed on her butt on top of my open backpack. "Ow."

"Jeez, are you okay?" If that had been me, I would have needed another trip to the hospital.

"Yes. I think." She lifted one of my many T-shirts up from under her. "Your clothes broke my fall."

My guava rolled out of the sleeve and across the floor.

"You found it! You're my hero!" I squealed.

She picked it up and tossed it into my hand. "Can we get back to you loving my brother, please?"

"Right. Is that bad?"

She broke out into the biggest smile I have ever seen. Pretty impressive for someone who just fell off a bed. Then she shrieked: "We're going to be sisters-in-law!"

I started taking faster breaths. Bigger breaths. Trying to. Couldn't breathe. Needed air. "But. What. If. It." I wheezed. "Doesn't . . . work out?"

She put her arm around me. "Linds, take a deep breath, okay?"

I tried. From our window, we could hear people laughing outside.

"If it doesn't work out, then it doesn't work out. You break up. You can't live your life afraid of things breaking down."

"But . . . that's what I do." That's what I've always done, I realized. I've lived my entire life in fear of breaking my legs. My toe. My heart.

But for good reason. "But I did break my toe," I mumbled to myself.

She raised an eyebrow. "Huh?"

"I mean, what if it doesn't work out? What if we break up? What if I break his heart or he breaks mine and then I can't be your maid of honor anymore?"

She nodded and carefully considered my point. I love that she knew exactly what I meant. "We'll have to consciously try to keep our relationship separate from your relationship. It's complicated. But doable. There's a difference between being careful and being afraid."

"Yeah?"

"Didn't you come on this vacation to learn to take risks?"

I nodded.

"So what are you waiting for?" she asked. "Go tell him."

Becca said he was still out with the rest of the group. I didn't want to leave the premises hunting for him in case I somehow missed him, so instead I parked myself on the tattered couch in the lobby. My heart was thumping like rain against a window. I guava-fied to calm myself down. Maybe my guava had stayed hidden until I had found the person worthy of being kissed.

Oh God! I see them. Hear them. Penny's giggles. Max's

and Kristin's camera flashes. I can see him through the glass door. I feel sick. Afraid. Should I run? Hide? Can I do this?

*Saturday, July 21, No-Clue-What-Time-It-Is-Since-We're-Crossing-Time-Zones-Again P.M.*

I've already had three glasses of airplane apple juice and I desperately have to pee. But I don't want to move.

Tommy's sleeping with his head on my knee. The plane is relatively empty, so we have a row to ourselves. Becca and Harold are in the seats in front of us. They've already made plans to meet up over Labor Day weekend. They're going to try long distance.

I hope they make it.

Sorry I haven't written . . . but I've been, well, too busy to write.

When Tommy finally walked into the lobby, I thought my heart would explode.

"What are you doing?" he asked.

"Waiting . . . for you," I mumbled. "Can we talk outside?"

He looked confused, obviously, since we had barely spoken since Bastille Day. But he shrugged, said good night to (a disappointed-looking) Penny, and motioned me to the door.

We walked down the beach and over to the water without talking.

We sat down on the rocks, our feet out in front of us. The

stars were out in full force and their light reflected in the water and against the darkness of the rocks.

"I . . . I . . ." I was terrified. Frozen. I had no idea what I was supposed to say.

He reached over and tapped my broken toe. "How is it?"

"It hurts," I said. "But I'll live." I thought about what he had asked me about on Bastille Day. About why I was so obsessed with having a fling. "You were right," I said, staring ahead at the lapping water. "I was afraid." I felt his eyes on me and turned toward him. "I wanted to have a fling to prove to myself that I could take risks. Which is dumb. Since it's relationships that scare the crap out of me."

"I know," he said softly.

I looked at his strong chin, and his big eyes, and his tasty lips. His broad shoulders . . . carrying a backpack around certainly agreed with him. Hey. Who knew? American boys could be pretty hot, too. I inched closer to him. "I'm kind of a scaredy-cat if you want to know the truth."

His turn to inch closer to me. "Are you afraid now?"

My palms were sweaty and my heart was going haywire but I felt pretty confident it wasn't from fear. "No," I said. "Are you?"

He grinned. "Well, the last time I tried to kiss you, I ended up on the pavement. And these rocks don't exactly look softer."

I laughed. And then I thought, what the hell. And I went

117

for it. I closed the space between us in under a second and kissed him. Brave, huh?

And the kiss was perfect. It started gently. His lips were soft and smooth. It was weird for the first few seconds — I kept thinking, omigod I'm kissing Tommy! — but then I stopped thinking entirely and we were *kissing* and his hands were on the back of my neck and mine were in his hair and on his back and under his shirt and . . . well, it was good.

Until he suddenly pulled away.

I panicked. He had changed his mind? He didn't really like me! I wasn't a good kisser. I had bit his tongue! "What's wrong?" I forced myself to say.

"A rock has buried itself into my elbow." With a grin, he plucked a pebble from his arm.

I laughed. With relief. "You scared me. I thought . . ."

"Thought what? That I was going to change my mind about you?"

I shrugged, feeling small and scared. "Maybe."

"I've liked you for ten years, Lindsay. Do you really think you're getting rid of me that easily?" He peeled himself off the beach and helped me up. "Are you okay to walk?"

I took his hand. "Definitely. I know a great lookout where we can watch the sunrise."

We walked, stopping occasionally to kiss, and talked. About relationships. About my mom. About his parents' divorce. About being afraid. About being brave. About how happy Becca was going to be. About French cheese.

We finally walked back into the hotel, holding hands, at six thirty the next morning. And held hands at breakfast. We held hands on the train to Monte Carlo. We held hands at the good-bye banquet dinner in Monte Carlo. We held hands on the train back to Nice. We held hands while saying good-bye to Pierre. We held hands during takeoff. Max and Kristin took pictures.

The lights in the plane just went out. I can't believe the trip is over. It went by so fast. I'm going to miss everything. The cheese. The trains. I think I might even miss Joanna's singing. But I'm also happy to be going home, fling in tow.

Hah. Fling. Who am I kidding? I may have gone looking for a fling but what I found is so much better.

*C'est la vie!*

# CABIN
# FEVER

By Erin Haft

# Prologue: The Bombshell

*Again with the drama . . .*

Molly Walker tried not to roll her eyes as she stumbled groggily into her family's sunlit kitchen. Once again, for the third straight morning, her little sister, Dakota, was sobbing at the breakfast table. And once again, Mom and Dad were huddled on either side of her, wearing their "Yes, our younger daughter is a freakish hybrid of everything wrong with Paris Hilton, but we still owe it to ourselves to be concerned" faces.

Funny: Molly could have pirouetted across the floor, her brown curls tied in a satin bow instead of hanging in her eyes, dolled up in a pink taffeta gown instead of ratty flannel pajamas, and not a single one of them would have noticed. But when drama involved the faux-blond, faux-blue-eyed Dakota Walker (and who *still* wore colored contacts?), the universe came to a screeching halt.

"Morning, everyone," Molly said, heading for the fridge.

Nobody answered. Classic.

No need to get in a snit, though. As of tomorrow, she would be long gone from this Dakota-obsessed nuthouse, on a bus to Camp Menominee in Vermont — which, summer by summer, was starting to feel a lot more like her real home. A faraway place smelling of fir trees and bug spray, a place where she belonged, where there was no fashion self-consciousness, no putting up with a wannabe BCBG model whose favorite saying was "I can't be bothered with chores, ya heard?"

No doubt about it; over the past six years, Molly's four weeks at Camp Menominee had changed from fun-filled jaunts into desperate escapes required for sanity.

Of course, there was also the *feel* of the place, so different from here — the memories of giggly walks through the pine forest with her friend Jess Schwartz, the chaos of "free swim" in Lake Ely, the Sunday night bonfires with fireflies dancing among sparks under the starry sky . . .

But most important, there was also the matter of a certain boy.

A boy named River. River Nicholas Ween. What a name. Rock star material? Or adorable geek material? Maybe both. A smile of anticipation flitted across Molly's face. It had been precisely eleven months and two days (not that she was counting) since she'd last seen him. Had he grown taller? Were his legs still tanned and perfect under those perennial cutoff shorts? Did his shaggy black hair still flop in just the right way? The questions to be answered. . . . And now that they were both eighteen and this might be their last summer together at camp, they could maybe turn those flirtatious glances into —

"My boyfriend!" Dakota wailed. "He's, like, totally moved on!"

Mom and Dad patted Dakota's shoulders.

Molly stifled a groan. They *couldn't* take Dakota seriously anymore. This emotional outpouring, this tragic three-day breakfast-table vigil . . . all of it was over some goofy high school sophomore named "Dark." Dakota had only dated him for four weeks. Plus, Molly knew for a fact that Dark's real name was Moses Steinberg. He'd nicknamed himself at about the same time he'd announced to the world (i.e. his eight MySpace friends) he'd decided to become a famous rapper. Then he'd dumped Dakota for some new faux-blond-of-the-month. Ah, to be fifteen again.

"I was doing my stomach series," Dakota continued, sniffling. "I put the iPod on shuffle. You know what came up first? 'Ain't It Good to Be a Gangsta.' It was our song!"

Molly yawned extra-loud and opened the fridge.

"Please, Mol," Dad scolded.

A "Hi, Mol" would have been nice. Or a "Sleep well, Mol?" Or maybe a "We're so proud of you, Mol, and thanks for setting a good example for your sister by graduating near the top of your class instead of scouring *Glamour* for the latest dye-preserving shampoo, and have a great time at camp before college starts." But no. *"Please, Mol."*

"Do you want some tomato juice, honey?" Mom whispered, gently stroking Dakota's highlights. "Hardly any calories. That might make you feel better."

Molly had to admit, there was something priceless about

this mother-daughter moment: mother in sweats, daughter in Adidas-by-Stella-McCartney jog bra. But then, there was also something priceless about the *cost* of said jog bra. And about Dakota's credit card debt in general. In fact, the priceless-ness in this kitchen was getting a little *too* priceless. New plan: grab coffee, run upstairs, and maybe leave for camp now.

Dad cleared his throat. "Mol, why don't you get some juice for your sister, okay?"

Molly removed a carton of milk and closed the refrigerator door.

"Mol?" Dad repeated. "Some tomato juice for your sister?"

"Oh, I'm sorry," Molly answered sweetly. "Were you talking to me, Dad? I slept great, thanks. How about you?" She strolled over to the coffeemaker and poured a large cup and added lots of sugar. "Listen, I'd love to chat, but I have to pack for camp. The bus leaves at five A.M. tomorrow, remember? Oh, hi, Dakota. I didn't see you there."

Mom and Dad sighed. Dakota sniffled again. Impressive. The girl could cry for hours, and her mascara would somehow never run. She did know her beauty products. All that time buried in *Glamour* had paid off. Molly hurried for the door.

"Wait a second, Mol," Dad called after her.

"What?"

"We have some news. Er, well . . . Dakota has some news."

Molly hesitated and frowned over her shoulder. "News?"

Dakota smiled through her tears. "Yeah. I'm coming to Camp Menominee with you this year. I'm gonna be a CIT — Counselor-in-Training. It's a loser move, I know, but I have to do *something* to get over Dark. And actually, you can help me pack. I'm still too devastated." She wiped her eyes. "Hey, they have a Gucci up there, right? Like at a mall or something? I saw this bracelet in their catalog that I loved. And it's weird, cuz usually I *hate* Gucci."

# I: The Bus Ride From Hell

**<u>Essential Items</u>**

**Hiking boots (broken in)**

**Bug spray**

**First aid kit**

**Flashlight**

**Rope**

**Sunscreen**

**Compass**

Molly gripped the list, hands trembling. She felt dizzy. The bus's rocking motions didn't help. Nor did the predawn darkness outside; it transformed every passenger window into a horror-film mirror. Everywhere Molly looked, she saw a reflection of her sister — perfectly made up, hair done and dyed (a $135 job!), in a mauve Juicy Couture slip dress — *on her way to Camp Menominee.*

"You didn't pack any of these things?" Molly croaked at last.

Dakota shrugged, rubbing her bleary eyes. "I couldn't be bothered. I don't get this list at all, Mol. It doesn't make any sense. There aren't any labels."

"Any what?"

"Nothing is branded. Which *brand* of hiking boots? They can't all be the same. I'm sure there's the Diane von Furstenberg of hiking boots, and I'm sure there's the Payless generic. You should have told me. You know the difference. Anyway, I can just borrow from you. I'm having a crisis, remember? You said you'd pack for me."

"I did not! You asked me, and I didn't even answer —"

"Look, Mol, I know you're anxious about seeing Nature Boy . . . Ocean or . . . whatever. But you don't have to take it out on me."

"His name is River," Molly corrected in a flat voice. Then she checked over her shoulder to make sure no one had heard. "And I'm not anxious."

Dakota grinned. "Please. You're crushing. Don't deny it. All spring long, I saw you trying to write him all those letters, then throwing them all away. You were writing the letters by *hand*, too. That's, like, a telltale sign of major crushing. Nobody writes letters by hand."

"He doesn't have e-mail," Molly muttered, turning away. "I told you, he's the son of the camp's owners. He lives up in the boondocks year-round. So I had to write him by hand. And, it's hard. When was the last time *you* wrote a letter by hand?"

"Honestly, I don't even e-mail anymore." Dakota yawned and picked at a manicured nail. "I'm strictly text-message. Although, FYI, Dark broke up with me via text. Totally inexcusable! Some things you have to do in person. Can you believe it?"

*I'm shocked,* Molly thought drily, but she kept her mouth shut.

Luckily Dakota seemed done with conversation too. She'd probably exhausted herself, complaining about the five A.M. departure time. ("I don't get why I can't just skip this 'Kick-off Breakfast' or whatever-it-is and get to camp in time for dinner," she'd whined approximately four zillion times.) Best just to maintain silence.

Molly shoved the list of forgotten items into her pocket. Soon they'd be arriving at the Madison Junction bus depot, the last real vestige of civilization before the wilds of Vermont. Of course, the word "civilization" might be pushing it as far as Madison Junction was concerned: The town consisted of little more than a snack shack and a post office. She smiled to herself, imagining the crazy, familiar scene: Sunrise in the parking lot, with all the first-time campers saying good-bye amid the chaos of unloading trunks and fishing tackle and sleeping bags . . . and the returning CITs and counselors, reconnecting with shrieks and hugs, punctuated by the grand appearance of River's parents, Belinda and Harris Ween, screeching up in their ancient bus, ready to whisk everyone off to Camp Menominee.

For a brief instant, Molly wondered what Dakota would make of the Weens — a graying hippie couple with perma-grins and glassy eyes that maybe betrayed a little too much "experimentation" in their youths. Maybe Dakota would freak out. Maybe she would have a nervous breakdown once she learned that there wasn't a Gucci even *remotely* near Madison Junction or Camp Menominee. Maybe she'd insist on jumping back on the bus and being rushed home to catch up on her beauty sleep.

Maybe?

Molly could always hope.

## II: Boho BFFs

"Mol! Over here!"

*Oh, God, no.* Molly froze as she helped Dakota with her trunk. It hit the blacktop with a loud *thwack*. This was one of those moments, one Molly had envisioned, one that should have been perfect: meeting up with Jess Schwartz in the Madison Junction depot parking lot! Molly and Jess had first been bunk mates six years ago and bunk mates every summer since, then CITs together, and now they were going to be co-counselors in charge of their own cabin — the Sparrow Cabin, for first-time overnighters, just like they'd once been.

And Molly knew if Dakota weren't there, she and Jess would already be hugging each other and apologizing for not having kept in touch more during the school year, then scrambling off to the Snack Shack to catch up on gossip before the Weens picked them up . . . but all Molly could do was stand there and gape.

"Mol?" Jess said again. She brushed a lone strand of black hair out of her eyes and hurried over to give Molly a quick squeeze. The fact that she was wearing a Camp Menominee T-shirt should have filled Molly with nostalgia; now it only made her want to dive under the bus. "Hello, Mol?" she said, wrinkling her freckled nose. "Hello? It's me. Remember? Were you lobotomized this spring?"

"My sister doesn't travel well," Dakota chimed in with a perky smile. "You should have seen her on this one car trip we took to Disney World. She barfed, like, the entire way — Oh, I'm sorry. I'm Dakota Walker. You are . . . ?"

Jess's eyes widened. She shot another baffled grin at Molly. "I'm Jess. You're the famous sister, huh? I've heard about you."

"Oh, I've heard about you too! You and Mol are, like, Boho BFFs!"

131

Molly opened her mouth and closed it. What could she possibly say? *Jess, I am so sorry. I should have gotten in touch the second I learned the twisted creature beside me was coming to camp this summer too. But I've been in a state of shock. Maybe I just don't want to believe it.*

"Yep, that's me and your sis," Jess replied good-naturedly. "Boho BFFs. We don't even shave our armpits."

"Eww!" Dakota cried.

Jess laughed again. "Kidding." She paused, eyeing Dakota's dress in the early morning sunshine. "Wow. You must have just come from a debutante ball or something."

"Oh, no, nothing like that," Dakota said, clearly missing the not-so-subtle dig. "I just want to make a good impression. Plus, I'm in a bad funk right now, and certain outfits make me feel better."

"A bad funk? What's that, like a seventies-theme costume party?"

Dakota sighed. "I wish." (*Was she even listening?*) "My boyfriend broke up with me. I thought we were in love too. His name is Dark."

"Actually, his name is Moses Steinberg," Molly grumbled. "Hey, Jess, want to go grab some coffee with me? I can explain everything —"

"Mol?" Dakota interrupted, her glossy lips curling in a pout. "I'm telling the story of why I'm going to this crunchy camp of yours instead of being with Dark. Besides, every

132

rapper has an alias. You know what Ad Rock's real name is? So why don't you let me talk to Jess and you can get us *all* some coffee." She reached for her Fendi bag and began fishing for her wallet. "I'll keep an eye on our stuff. I need some quality face time with your BFF anyway. She can give me all the juicy deets about this Nature Boy you're obsessed with."

"Wait, you mean River?" Jess asked.

Molly's jaw tightened. "I'm not obsessed with him. He's a *friend*."

"If he's just a friend, then can I snag him? I could use a cute rebound." Dakota smiled wickedly and arched an eyebrow, handing over a mottled Visa card. "Oh, and can you make sure mine has non-dairy cream? You can put it on my tab."

"It's not *your* tab," Molly hissed through clenched teeth. "It's Mom and Dad's."

"So why not max it out? Then I won't be able to use it anymore."

Jess burst out laughing. "The girl's got a point, Mol. I'll take some non-dairy cream, too, if you don't mind."

"I . . . I . . ." Molly's eyes darted between Jess and her sister. "Fine." She snatched the credit card away. "But Jess? While I'm gone, please use this 'face time' to tell my sister why she should have brought bug spray. Tell her the 'deets' about the mosquitoes."

"I'd rather hear about the boy," Dakota muttered.

"I'd rather *talk* about the boy," Jess admitted.

They both laughed.

*Argh!* Stifling a scream, Molly stormed across the parking lot.

Okay. She couldn't allow herself to get so upset. For whatever unfathomable reason, Dakota was part of Camp Menominee life now. Molly would just have to deal. But what was up with Jess? Jess *knew* about Dakota: how unscrupulous she was, how she lived for one-upping Molly in the social department. And . . . as close as Molly was to Jess, Jess didn't know how Molly really felt about River. Jess hardly paid any attention to him, precisely because he was Weens' son. The parental connection had always been a turnoff for her. ("A River fling is a bad call," Jess had giggled from the top of their bunk beds late one night last summer. "It'd be like hooking up with the principal's kid.") So where did she get off talking about him? She'd never led a nature hike with him up Mount Green; she'd never splashed around Lake Ely with him; she'd never sat beside him as he strummed his guitar at the Sunday night bonfire, singing along to the old-time classic: *"Let me be your salty dog, or I won't be your man at all . . . Honey, let me be your salty dog . . ."*

So on the other hand — maybe Jess *should* talk about him. Right. Because that way, once they arrived at camp, Dakota wouldn't pay any attention to him either. She'd never use him as a rebound. He liked folk music, not rap. He wore second-hand clothes, not "brands." Best of all, he didn't have an alias.

Molly smiled at the thought, her heart fluttering. He didn't need one.

## III: Choose Your Own Way, Be It Swimming, Hiking, or Macramé!

"That's River, Dakota," Jess whispered excitedly. "What do you think?"

"Oh my God, he's way hotter than I thought," Dakota breathed. She squinted at him through the crowded tables of the Camp Menominee Rec Hall. "Either that or I'm *totally* sleep deprived. I should have worn my prescription shades. My contacts are no good up here. I forgot my saline solution."

"Yeah, I was wondering why your eyes turned from blue to green," Jess teased.

Dakota stuck her tongue out at her. They both started cracking up.

*This is a nightmare,* Molly thought, shredding her napkin.

Somehow, in less than two hours, Dakota had not only managed to swipe half the belongings from Molly's trunk (including her sunblock), she'd also managed to swipe Molly's best friend. It was ridiculous. Even though Jess was brilliant and hilarious, and Dakota was . . . Dakota, they seemed to get

135

along perfectly. To make matters worse, the Weens had assigned Dakota to be the CIT for *their* cabin, Sparrow Cabin. To add proverbial insult to injury, Dakota had asked Jess to share bunk beds ("Molly snores") and Jess had agreed. In short, they had left Molly in the dust to form a chatty new-and-improved "BFF" duo — and all before eight A.M. Amazing. Socially one-upped again.

And now, here they were at the traditional Camp Menominee Kick-off Breakfast, waiting for Belinda and Harris Ween to introduce themselves to the newcomers. And it should have been a blast, munching on those soggy blueberry pancakes with the girls of Sparrow Cabin — Kim, Lily, Sasha, Jen, and Sophie — cute little ten-year-olds, with their braces and bobbed hair, whispering nervously to one another. Dakota barely showed any interest in the girls, even though she would be semi-responsible for them for the next four weeks.

Molly took a deep breath. She caught a whiff of the dewy pine trees outside, mingling with the woodsy aroma of the Rec Hall and the scent of baked goods and maple syrup. *Yes.* Calming. Relaxing. She shoved the napkin shreds into her pockets. This was Camp Menominee. Home-away-from-home. She would not let her little sister ruin her summer. Besides, Dakota was right: River did look hot.

Actually, that was an understatement. He stood next to his parents, smiling that killer mellow smile, in a flannel shirt over a worn white thermal. His dark bangs had grown. His cutoffs hung low. His legs were even tanner than she remembered.

Molly could feel herself blushing.

"Hello, newbies!" River's mom announced. A hush fell over the tables. "May I have your attention, please? As you know, I am Belinda Ween. Thank you for joining the Camp Menominee family! As you'll soon discover, things are very relaxed here; we don't have many rules. We ask that you be kind to those around you. We ask you to look out for one another and pitch in and help out when needed. Other than that . . ." She took a deep breath and, together, every returning CIT and counselor chanted: "Choose your own way, be it swimming, hiking, or macramé!"

The Rec Hall erupted in applause. River rolled his eyes at Molly through the crowd as he clapped, as if to say: *My parents really need to update their material.* Molly's pulse picked up a beat. It was the first time they'd made eye contact since she'd arrived. She'd forgotten how big and bright and blue his were. *Natural* blue.

"Macramé?" Dakota yawned. "What's that, like a B-list-celebrity fragrance?"

The girls of Sparrow Cabin giggled.

Molly's lips tightened. River's mom's speech may have been a little hackneyed, but it *was* tradition. And Camp

Menominee was all about tradition. Not that Dakota knew or cared. No, she definitely wasn't CIT material. Or River Nicholas Ween material for that matter either.

## IV: Guess Who's a Summer Dish?

It wasn't until late afternoon, in the paint-splattered bedlam of the Arts & Crafts shed, that Molly finally connected with River — as in, had actual verbal communication. Not that her first contact with River was anything to write home about. Not that she ever intended to write home about River anyway.

"So how come you never told us that you were dragging your little sister up here, Mol?" River asked, casually tying his flannel shirt around his waist.

Molly swallowed. "I . . ." She had no clue how to respond. Why couldn't River have pulled her aside in the Rec Hall this morning? Why did he have to wait until the end of the day to track her down, when her hair was a damp mess from splashing around in the lake with the Sparrow Cabin (Dakota had refused to jump in, of course), her cutoffs were soggy (she hadn't had time to change out of her bathing suit), and her flip-flops were all squishy? Most egregious, why did the very first words River spoke to her — after eleven months and three days (not that she was counting) — have to be about Dakota?

Molly's brain squirmed with a dozen other inane thoughts as she sat there. *Jess and I really should be keeping an eye on our campers. Did River's skin always smell this good? Lily probably shouldn't be handling those big cutting shears unsupervised. Jess is annoying me. Is that a hole in the roof? The Weens could use some more paintbrushes —*

"Sorry, sweetie, Molly's got a lot on her mind right now," Dakota piped up. Her gaze flickered toward the clay table where three girls from Sparrow Cabin were building a sloppy, dangerous-looking construction entirely out of glue and tongue depressors. "Check the madness, FYI." She gave him a big smile.

River grinned back. "FYI?"

"For-your-information? Text-speak?" She raised her eyebrows. "Oh, but that's right. You people don't even have Internet access here. What's up with that?"

"Well, it *is* camp," River replied. "My parents prefer things a little rustic."

Dakota scrunched her eyebrows. "I don't get it. A little . . . what?"

"Old-fashioned. No Internet, no cell phones, no TV —"

"No cell phones?" Dakota interrupted. "Says who?" She reached into her bag and pulled out hers. "Hell-o-o-o?"

He shrugged. "Well, sure, you can bring them. You just won't get service."

Dakota's face fell. She frowned, jabbing furiously at the keypad. "Oh, my God, you're right. I'm totally out of range. Horror story!"

River's smile widened. "If you want to talk actual horror stories, I'm a pro."

Dakota's eyes narrowed as she shoved her phone back in her bag, but she was smiling too. In fact, both smiles were a little overly friendly, Molly thought, especially for two people who'd just met, with zero in common.

"Hey, Dakota, would you mind taking those big shears away from Lily?" Molly asked. "I'm worried she's going to hurt herself."

"Oh, I'm sure Lily's fine," Dakota murmured, not even bothering to look. "I want to hear more about these horror stories. River?"

He stroked his chin with exaggerated concern. "Well, for starters, don't wear a bikini in the lake. It's ice cold, and the jellyfish are vicious. I'd wear a wet suit. A couple of skinny CITs nearly froze solid last year. Also, stay away from the soccer field. The rattlesnake holes can break your legs if you fall in. . . . What else? Oh yeah, the boathouse is haunted. And infested with rabid squirrels. And keep your cabin windows closed, because a new species of tarantula migrated to Vermont, and they can burrow through the screens. And that's pretty much it, except for . . . The Summer Dishes."

*The Summer Dishes!* Molly's stomach squeezed. *Oh, God.*

Until now, *she'd* been smiling. But she'd forgotten about The Summer Dishes. Or maybe she'd just repressed the memory. Jess nudged her. She scowled back.

Dakota chuckled. "You're such a liar, River."

"You think? I'll see you at breakfast tomorrow." He sauntered toward the door. "I gotta go. I've got my own cabin, FYI. Eagle Cabin. And I sort of don't trust my CIT. His name is Guido. I'm not joking. What sort of parent would name their kid — ?"

"River?" Dakota cut in with a smirk.

"Funny. Very funny."

"Hey, how old is Eagle Cabin?" she called after him.

He paused. "Same age as Sparrow Cabin. And I'm the only senior counselor. It's sort of a crazy story. My cocounselor got mono. But my parents figured that I could handle the counselor duties on my own, because I practically grew up here —"

"Yeah, yeah, TMI," Dakota said impatiently. "But I'm thinking: Can our cabin and your cabin plan an overnight together? Jess says you guys do boy-girl overnights all the time. You know, like, if the cabins are the same age group."

River turned to Molly. "Um . . . sure. Our cabins could camp out together on Mount Green. Maybe next week? Monday? After the first bonfire? Mol?"

"Why not?" Molly tried to force a smile. "Sounds great."

"Awesome. It's a date." River shot one last puzzled smile at Dakota, then hurried out into the late afternoon sunshine, his flannel shirt flapping in the breeze.

*It* is *a date, isn't it?* Molly thought, growing more miserable by the second.

Dakota sighed and rested her head on Jess's shoulder. "What a hottie. And funny too! You never told me Nature Boy was so hot and funny, Mol."

"Ah, he's old news," Jess muttered. "I'm more curious about this Guido guy. Frankly, I could use a fling with a younger man. I like the dangerous type."

"Eww! What if he's, like, some greasy wannabe *Soprano* mob dude?" Dakota whispered. "But for real, Mol, what *are* The Summer Dishes?"

Good question. And Molly could have told Dakota the truth. She could have explained it all: "The Summer Dishes" referred to a goofy tradition (Camp Menominee *was* all about tradition) where a mysterious culprit (Molly was pretty sure it was River, though he denied it every year) snuck into the Rec Hall on the second night of camp and erased the breakfast menu from the chalkboard — and in the place of, say, veggie sausage and egg whites, this culprit scrawled the name of one new girl CIT and one new guy CIT (always the best-looking) . . . and somehow, that girl and guy always seemed to end up being the most popular at camp. It was too depressing. Let Dakota figure it out.

"Like River said, you'll see at breakfast tomorrow," Molly grumbled. "Now will you please take those shears away from Lily?"

# V: Five Summers Down the Drain, But Fine

There was a term for this kind of unhappiness: "Murphy's Law." It was a cliché, but accurate: *Whatever can go wrong, will go wrong.* Molly had known what was coming. How could she not know? Still, it stung. No, it *more* than stung to see the chalkboard in the Rec Hall at breakfast the next morning.

THEY KNOW THEY'RE THE SUMMER DISHES:
DAKOTA WALKER AND GUIDO FALCONE

As per tradition, every single camper and counselor hooted and cheered, even the newcomers. The girls of Sparrow Cabin hooted and cheered the loudest of all. Of course they did: Dakota was their CIT. Cabin pride! Jess cheered right along with them. And River's parents shook their heads as always, and River stood beside them, smiling that same inscrutable, mellow smile. But the worst part? The part Molly hated to admit to herself? Just like every year, she wondered what it might feel like to see *her* name up there. And deep down, she knew it probably wouldn't feel so bad.

"What's going on?" Dakota whispered. She blushed and grabbed Molly's arm, pulling her close. "What does it mean?"

Molly sighed and studied her organic grain waffles. "It means you're a star. It means Camp Menominee belongs to you and Guido."

"Really? Wow! So do we get to change some stuff? Like the bugle wake-up thing, reveille or whatever? It goes off *way* too early —"

"I don't mean camp literally belongs to you," Molly groaned. "I just mean . . . actually, forget it. Try to change whatever you want. I need some coffee." She wrenched her arm from Dakota's grasp and hurried toward the coffee line.

"Hey, Mol?" Dakota called after her. "Sorry! What did I say? But it reminded me: Did you ever see that chick-in-the-army movie with Goldie Hawn? Seriously, she was so cute in that! She, like, totally took charge. I could be, like, totally Goldie. . . ."

Molly's throat tightened. Fortunately, the continuing applause drowned out Dakota's voice. Molly planted herself in line at the ancient coffee urn, trying to ignore the winks and grins of her fellow campers and counselors, though she knew exactly what those winks and grins meant. *Your sister is the bomb, Mol! You've been talking about Dakota all these years, but now that we're seeing her in person — whoa!*

Whatever. Molly made herself an extra sugary cup of coffee, then stomped back to the Sparrow Cabin table. Ah, Murphy's Law, indeed. Her seat had been taken by River himself. He was busy forking up bites of organic grain waffles — from Molly's plate, no less — his eyes glued to Dakota.

144

"Mol, you never told me your little sister was such a movie buff," he said, his mouth half-full.

Molly slurped from her mug. Her eyes flashed between Dakota and River, and then to Jess and the rest of her campers, who were all digging into their food. She could feel an explosion building inside.

"I'm not that much of a movie buff," Dakota replied in Molly's silence. She smiled up at Molly, her porcelain features highlighted by makeup. Molly's head began to spin. *Makeup! At camp! And that skirt! It's a Dolce and Gabbana!* "But the reason this subject came up, Mol, is because I'd lay off the java. I'm not kidding. For real, it leads to depression. We were just talking about this black-and-white movie with the guys from the Wu-Tang Clan, and it was actually really funny but, like, informative. . . ."

"*Coffee and Cigarettes*," River said.

"Right!" Dakota beamed at him.

Molly blinked. "What?"

"The name of the movie Dakota was talking about." River smiled up at Molly, too, then dropped the fork on her plate and stood. "Sorry, I stole your seat. But I'm not going to apologize for eating your breakfast, because I know you never even *eat* breakfast. Although you should."

"That's what I'm saying!" Dakota threw up her hands. "Mol is all on my case for not having a compass or whatever, but *she* only drinks coffee in the morning. And when you're on

145

your feet for hours on end, chasing these little dudes around and making sure they don't kill themselves, breakfast is the most important meal of the day."

Almost as if on cue, the Sparrow Cabin girls started giggling.

"Yo, Riv!" a gruff voice shouted across the room. "Stop trying to hit on the ladies, son! We've got a situation!"

River's face flushed. So did Dakota's. Molly glanced toward the Eagle Cabin table. A tall, lanky blond boy in a backward Red Sox cap was frantically beckoning to River while trying to keep his campers from hurling pieces of waffle at one another.

"That's Guido," River muttered under his breath.

"He's *cute*," Jess whispered. "Definitely Summer Dish material."

Dakota clucked her tongue. "You think? The baseball cap thing is so over. Looks to me like he's seen a few too many episodes of *Growing Up Gotti.*"

River laughed and hurried back to his table. Molly looked from him to Dakota, then to Guido and Jess, then back to River. . . . And all of a sudden, a strange thing happened. As she watched River go, the anger inside her began to evaporate, like the fog off Lake Ely at sunrise. Why was she so upset, anyway? Yes, River was hot and funny and played guitar — but really, his beaded necklace was a little too Logan-from-*Veronica-Mars*. Plus, he needed a haircut. Plus she didn't know him that well. Four weeks a summer for six years . . . what was that? Not even six months total. How could she *know* him? She'd just built him up in her mind. Inside, he was probably exactly like every cocky boy from her high school back home. He was probably worse.

Right. Molly took a deep breath and smiled at Dakota. Let her littler sister have River if she wanted him. Her crush was officially over. She was free! Which meant she could focus on what was really important. She was a counselor now. *She* could take charge. She could be, "like, totally Goldie," as a certain someone might say.

"Uh, Mol, are you okay?" Dakota asked. "You're sort of wigging me out the way you're staring at me like that."

"Never better," Molly said, sipping from her mug. "Now let's finish up here, campers. We've got lots to do today."

# VI: Diary of a Madwoman?

While Molly had always admired the Weens' laissez-faire philosophy, it could occasionally lead to anarchy that verged on full-fledged disaster. So seeing that she was free of her River Nicholas Ween obsession (finally!), she decided to take some action. Her new mission was to provide some structure for the Sparrow Cabin.

That very night, after lights-out, Molly snuck out of her bunk and hurried down the dark wooded path to the Weens' ramshackle cottage beside the boathouse — and pounded on the door.

"Yes?" Mrs. Ween answered. She opened up in a bath-robe, her long gray hair billowing in every direction. "Molly?" She blinked over her bifocals. "What's wrong, dear? Is every-thing all right? It's after eleven."

Molly smiled, slapping a mosquito at her neck. "I'm sorry, everything's fine." She raised her voice to be heard over the crickets. "I was just wondering — do you have a schedule for camp activities? Like an hour-by-hour calendar sort of thing? I just really want to provide, you know, a *plan* for my campers. Some structure."

Mrs. Ween blinked again. "You sure everything's okay, honey? Do you have the flu? Were you bitten by a bug?"

"No . . . I . . ." Molly's hands fell to her sides. Maybe a part of her had been hoping that River would be here. But of course he wouldn't. He was the head counselor of Eagle Cabin. He was in his bunk, asleep. *Everyone* was asleep — except for crazies like her. Blood rushed to her face. This was a terrible mistake. "You know, on second thought, I think I can wing it, like always."

"No, hold on a moment dear," Mrs. Ween said. "You want a day planner, right?"

Molly heaved a sigh of relief. "Exactly."

"Well, I'm not sure if we have one of those, but I think we have something you could use. . . ." Mrs. Ween flashed an anxious smile. She disappeared down the hall, her robe swishing. "Just wait there."

For a brief instant, Molly considered bolting back to her cabin. But then she'd freak out Mrs. Ween even more, and the Weens would probably ask her to go home for psychiatric counseling. And a rumor would spread and grow into a Camp Menominee legend, about how Molly Walker went completely insane one summer and went on a violent rampage and maybe got mangled in a bear trap, and how River didn't even care, and how her ghost returned to haunt the Arts & Crafts shed or something. . . .

"Here you are. Hope this helps."

Molly swallowed. Mrs. Ween reappeared and handed her a beautiful old diary, leather bound with vellum pages, locked with a silver clasp.

"Wow," Molly said. "You sure this isn't like a family heirloom or anything?"

Mrs. Ween laughed. "Hardly. River bought it at a yard sale for two dollars."

"Oh. Well, thanks." Molly tried to ignore how her heart skipped at the sound of River's name. *I. Don't. Like. Him. Anymore.*

"No problem. And Molly, I just want to tell you, I am so happy your sister is part of the Camp Menominee family now." She fixed Molly with a curious stare. "Do you think she paid any mind to that 'Summer Dish' silliness?"

Molly's smile faltered. "Probably not so much. And thanks for this. I'll make sure it's put to good use."

Mrs. Ween nodded, her brow furrowing. "Of course, sweetheart." She paused. "Are you sure you're okay?"

"Yeah. Thanks again. Good night." Clutching the diary in both hands, Molly scurried back up the path to Sparrow Cabin, the moon and stars lighting her way.

# VII: Yes, Diary of a Madwoman

_Tuesday_

Tried to create some sort of schedule but failed. Wanted to go canoeing at 9 a.m. But when Dakota opened the life jacket bin in the boathouse, she saw a squirrel. She screamed so loudly that the girls ran away. Took me an hour to track down Sophie. She was hiding under her bunk bed. (I want to kill River.) Later that night, Dakota told Sophie that if "any rabid squirrel messes with the Sparrow Cabin, we'll mess right back. They can't stop me. I'm one of The Summer Dishes, right?" This is a direct quote. The girls cheered, including Jess.

## Wednesday

Hot day today. River dropped by the cabin before lights-out, to flirt with Dakota as far as I can tell. He told us to open the windows for cross-ventilation. "What about the tarantulas?" Dakota asked. He laughed. I think they made eyes at each other. Wanted to barf. Later, we tried to open the windows but they were broken and kept falling shut. Dakota used three maxed-out credit cards to prop them up a little. The girls cheered. Worst of all, it actually worked. There was a nice cool breeze. I hate my sister.

## Thursday

I really wish River hadn't opened his big mouth. Dakota convinced the girls that the chipmunk holes in the soccer field <u>are</u> rattlesnake holes. They refuse to go play soccer now, period. Spent most of the beautiful afternoon in the Arts & Crafts shed, where Dakota gave all the girls makeovers. The upside: I think she's finally out of makeup.

## Friday

Today Lily asked if Dakota and I were really sisters, or if I was adopted. Her exact words: "It's just that Dakota's so pretty. Oh! I didn't mean it like that! She's just really well put-together. You know? You don't look that much alike is all I'm saying." Note to self: okay for Lily to handle cutting shears unsupervised from now on.

151

Saturday

Another hot day. Eagle Cabin attacked us with water guns. Guido led the charge. Does Jess really like him? To quote Dakota: Eww! Speaking of my sister, she wore a white Juicy top — "It's the weekend; I have to look nice." River made sure to give her a good hosing-down. Not sure how to feel. Happy on one hand that he nearly ruined her $150 shirt, unhappy that he wanted to catch a glimpse of what was underneath.

Sunday

Pouring rain this morning. Bonfire canceled. Actually relieved. I'm sure Dakota would somehow steal my usual spot next to River, and snuggle with him while he plays guitar, and request "Ain't It Good to Be a Gangsta," and then wait until everyone leaves and roast a s'more with him and then make out with him and marry him and they'll become the next Mr. and Mrs. Ween.

Later Sunday

Good news: The weather is clearing. Bonfire = back on! Supposed to be gorgeous tomorrow for the big overnight with Eagle Cabin too. Or is this all bad news? Will have to see River again. With Dakota. Oops. Just remembered I'm not supposed to care.

# VIII: Honey, Let Me Be Your Salty Dog

There was once a time when Sunday was Molly's favorite night of the week. Dinner was even more lax than usual, just grilled burgers and dogs served outside the Rec Hall, picnic-style, and "Bug Juice," some kind of frighteningly sweet red syrup that passed for a beverage. Campers could do as they pleased as the sun went down: hop in the lake, play Frisbee, hang out in their cabins . . . their only obligation was to present the Weens with a handwritten letter home by nightfall. That was their ticket to the Sunday night bonfire, the premier Camp Menominee event. No letter, no admission. It was the Weens' way of ensuring that campers maintained at least some kind of communication with their parents during the four weeks of free-for-all.

And until this very Sunday, Molly had always followed the same routine, ever since she was a first-time camper: She went for a quick dip, snagged a hot dog on the way back to her cabin, then changed into jeans and a sweatshirt and settled into bed to write Mom and Dad before flip-flopping off to the bonfire with Jess.

Only tonight she was suffering from major writer's block. Maybe she'd worn herself out with all that scribbling in her diary. She sat in her bunk, her eyes drifting from the blank stationery to Dakota — sitting cross-legged on the cabin floor with Sophie and Lily, trying to get *them* to write something, anything, so they could stick a piece of paper in an envelope and hand it over to the Weens.

"Come on, you guys, everybody else has written home!" Dakota urged. "It's easy. Listen, I stink at writing letters. Ask Mol. I hardly even know *how* to write a letter. But here's mine. You can pretty much copy it if you want." Dakota took a deep breath and held the sheet of paper in front of her eyes. "Dear Mom and Dad," she read. "How are you? I am fine. Well, not like *fine*, fine. I mean, first of all, there are like pine needles everywhere. I have them in my bed, in my clothes, even in my hair. Who knew Vermont had so many pine trees? Horror story! And FYI, bug spray doesn't work." Dakota broke off.

The girls sat up straight and immediately began to scrawl away, scrunching their foreheads in concentration. Dakota winked at Molly. "Easy, right?" she mouthed.

Molly swallowed, staring back at her own blank sheet of paper.

Yes. Easy. She bit her lip and drew a very large unhappy face:

☹.

Then she popped it in an envelope, addressed it, and shoved it in her jeans' pocket.

\* \* \*

The bonfire was held in a long-forgotten baseball field at the far edge of camp, a good fifteen-minute hike through the woods. As per tradition, once the sun was down and the moon was up, the counselors led their campers single-file down the uneven trail, their flashlight beams bouncing in the darkness, the mosquitoes buzzing, and the crickets chirping. The longer they hiked, the more the woods began to smell of smoke and the bugs began to disappear. Then, seemingly out of nowhere, the clearing appeared. There it was: a crackling fire of old plywood, in front of some rickety old bleachers. For the next three hours, every single member of the "Camp Menominee Family" would snuggle on those benches for a night of silly jokes and sing-alongs. Fun, fun, fun . . .

*Ugh.* Molly stood off to the side at the trail's end. She eyed River as Dakota, Jess, and the rest of the Sparrow Cabin girls handed their envelopes over to Mr. and Mrs. Ween. As usual, River sat front-row center. Tonight, of course, he was joined by Guido and the rest of his campers. No room there. Not that Dakota seemed discouraged. She didn't waste a second. She snapped off her flashlight and made a beeline straight for him.

"Can the girls and I sit next to you?" Dakota asked him, batting her lashes.

"Of course, of course." River glanced toward his campers. "Slide down, dudes. Make some room here." He hesitated, peering mock-flirtatiously down the row of girl campers as they crowded in beside him. "Say, would you ladies like to strum my guitar?" He gently handed the instrument to Dakota. "Run your fingers over the strings, then pass it down. Everyone gets a turn."

Molly stared as Dakota passed the instrument down, and the girls giggled and tried to strum, one by one, the guitar comically oversized in their laps. She felt worse than she had all week. Her pictograph letter home had summed it up. She knew she'd been lying to herself. River *wasn't* like the cocky schmucks back home. He was sweet, he was generous — and he was sitting next to Dakota.

Dakota handed the guitar back to him. "What happens now?" she asked.

"Now we sing 'Salty Dogs,'" he said, shooting a quick grin at Molly. She could barely hear him over the bonfire's cracking flames.

Dakota smirked. "What are 'Salty Dogs'?"

He chuckled. "They're sort of like little insults, done in limerick form. It's a Menominee tradition. You'll see."

"Don't you want to sit with your cabin?" Mrs. Ween whispered in Molly's ear.

"Uh . . . no thanks," Molly said. She folded her arms across her chest, the sleeves of her hoodie flopping. "It looks a little crowded. I think I'll just —"

Before she could finish her thought, River tapped out the rhythm on his guitar, and then began to strum. Everyone who knew the song joined in. Mr. and Mrs. Ween sang loudest of all: *"Let me be your salty dog . . . Or I won't be your man at all . . . Honey, let me be your salty dog . . ."* Normally Molly would have joined right in. Tradition! Now, she was silent.

Then came the pause. Who would go first? Who would poke fun of whom?

Jess raised her hand. Molly's shoulders sagged. Yep. Tradition. She was *sick* of tradition. Everyone cheered; then came the ceremonial holding-of-the-breath . . . then Jess unfolded a piece of paper in the flickering firelight and chanted:

*"There once was a girl named Dakota,*
*Who wanted more boys in her quota.*
*She asked her libido*
*Who answered: 'Duh, Guido'*
*Will she make him her 'Summer Dish' coda?"*

River laughed. "Get it now?"

"As if!" Dakota cried.

He started strumming again, grinning at Molly through the smoke, his eyes glittering in the sparks. Dakota clapped along. Molly sighed and turned away. She felt like bolting. But at least River didn't break into "Ain't It Good to Be a Gangsta." That was something. At least her real life wasn't the *complete* nightmare she'd imagined — just eerily and uncannily close.

Of course, there was always tomorrow's overnight trip.

## IX: Horror Story

"All right, ladies!" Guido shouted. "We got a lot of hiking ahead of us, so I don't want to hear any whining! Everybody fill up their canteens?"

*Ladies.* Molly squeezed her eyes shut. Guido had to call his boy campers "ladies." Of course he did. The guy didn't have an original thought in his head. And Jess thought Guido was cute? *Sheesh.* Standing here at the base of Mount Green, surrounded by a bunch of people who had clearly gone insane, with nothing but a very long hike — two miles distance and a thousand feet vertical — until they reached the campsite, Molly honestly felt as if she should either run away or —

A finger poked her arm. She opened her eyes.

"Mol?" Guido asked, tightening his backpack straps. "You ready?"

"Uh . . . yeah." She glanced back toward her own campers, their faces eager in the mid-afternoon sun, exchanging curious smiles with the boys of Eagle Cabin. Jess was dutifully inspecting the boots of each girl (*the job I should be doing*, Molly thought with a pang of guilt), making sure the laces were tied properly, double-looped and double-knotted for extra support . . . and then Molly's eyes fell on Dakota's feet, bringing up the rear of the procession — in a pair of raffia metallic ballet flats.

Molly gulped. "Dakota?"

"Yeah?" her sister replied, dabbing some sunblock on her nose.

"What sort of hiking gear are you wearing?"

Dakota peered over the rims of her sunglasses. "Mol, it was either these or a pair of cork-soled Marc Jacobs platforms. Like I'm really gonna risk ruining *those* on some overnight through the woods? I'm saving those for the dance."

River stood beside Dakota, shaking his head and chuckling.

Molly blinked at the both of them. "I guess . . . you're right," she managed. "What can I say? Good choice."

"Thanks!" Dakota answered brightly. The Sparrow Cabin girls nodded their approval. She tucked the sunblock tube back in her skirt pocket. "Now, there's one thing I want to cover before we go. I mean, I know you have your new schedule book thingy or whatever, but if there are too many bugs, can we turn back?"

For nearly the thousandth time in the past week, her little sister had rendered her speechless. Molly opened her mouth. No words would come.

"Don't worry, babe," Guido replied. He tilted his baseball cap in a way that was probably meant to be seductive but looked more like some parody of a third-rate hip-hop video. "I got plenty of extra bug spray."

\*　　\*　　\*

Surprise, surprise: It took less than an hour and thirty-three minutes (not that Molly was counting) for the newest Dakota Walker drama to kick in.

"Oh, my God, you guys!" Dakota shrieked. "Ow! I'm really, really hurt!"

*Here we go.* Molly turned and peered back down the trail, where Dakota had planted herself on a tree stump and had begun massaging her right ankle. All ten campers from the Eagle and Sparrow cabins rushed to her. Molly couldn't quite bring her feet to move, though. She *had* been leading the hike — warning Dakota about errant bugs, pointing out hidden roots, clearing the brush . . . but none of that mattered, because Menominee's newest Summer Dish was in trouble. *Horror story!*

"I think I twisted something," Dakota moaned, wincing. She shook her flat into the dirt. "Ugh. Maybe the cork soles would have been a better call."

"Just try to hold it still," Jess said. She knelt down and examined Dakota's leg. "It doesn't seem to be cut or scraped or anything, so that's good."

River crouched beside her. So did Guido. In fact, everyone except Molly was now huddled around Dakota — staring at her flawless, tanned, nail-polished foot. Funny. From where Molly stood, her sister's ankle didn't even look swollen. No, from where Molly stood, it looked as though Dakota was about to receive a pedicure from a bunch of ten-year-olds in hiking boots. And her former best friend. And a blond wannabe gangsta who made Dark look like Brad-Pitt-meets-Einstein.

And the boy she once thought was the only one for her . . .

"Hey, Mol, can you toss me your first-aid kit?" River called. He gently kneaded Dakota's lower calf, then lowered his voice. "Does it hurt when I do that, Dakota?"

Molly swallowed. Maybe she should just toss her entire backpack straight at River's head. Then he could dig through it and find the precious first-aid kit for himself.

"No, it doesn't hurt," Dakota muttered in the silence. "Uh, so I don't need first aid. I think I'll just go back and rest in my bunk bed. Anyway, walking down a mountain is easier than walking up, right?" She shook her leg free of River's hands. "But, thanks."

River's forehead wrinkled in concern. "Actually, that's not true. Hiking down a mountain is harder on your shins and ankles than hiking up."

Dakota giggled and slipped her flat back on. "Oh, come on, Nature Boy. I'll be fine. Like they said in *Wet Hot American Summer*, I'll 'walk it off.'"

Unbelievable. Molly almost laughed too. Dakota was faking. Obviously. She probably just wanted to go back to the cabin and take a nap — alone for once, without the girls fawning over her, begging for fashion tips or film quotes. The bug-bite plan didn't work, so she pretended to get hurt. But then, it wasn't all *that* unbelievable, was it? No less believable than anything else that had happened at camp so far . . .

"How're you gonna find your way without a compass?" Guido asked. "Even if your ankle's fine, sweetheart, these paths get tricky on the way down. You can get lost. The shadows can mess with you in the late afternoon. I should go with you."

Jess frowned at him. "I can go with her. I've got a compass."

"Well, if Mol had packed the Diane von Furstenberg of compasses for me, I'd be in great shape," Dakota put in drily, shooting a quick grin at her sister. "But no biggie. I don't need a compass. The sun sets in the west. Anybody who's ever seen any beach movie knows that. The sun is setting that way . . . which means camp is back *that* way."

Molly followed Dakota's gestures. Her eyes narrowed. Talk about unbelievable — way more than her sister's faux drama — Dakota was actually *right*.

"Then I say we both go, Jess," Guido suggested. He wriggled his eyebrows. "That way, in case Dakota falls again, or if she's hurt worse than she looks, she's got two healthy professionals to take her the rest of the way home. And I'm a Dish too."

*I don't even want to think about where you're going with that*, Molly thought queasily. "Well, if you both go, then we

162

might as well call off the overnight," she mumbled. She ambled back down the path, tugging on her backpack straps. "Come on, campers, let's head back —"

"Whoa, wait a sec," River interrupted. "Why call it off?"

Molly gazed into his dark-blue eyes. She tried to ignore how beautiful they were, sparkling under his black wavy hair. "Um, because we'll be two CITs and a cocounselor short?" she said in a flat voice.

"Yeah, but Guido's right. He and Jess can handle taking Dakota back to your cabin, and you and I can handle this. Come on, Mol, you're just as an experienced overnighter as I am. You've climbed Mount Green as many times as I have, maybe even more. Besides . . ." River glanced around at the boys and girls of Eagle and Sparrow cabins — the very kids Molly had obsessed over for the past week. She'd desperately tried to convince herself that these little ten-year-old campers were what she loved most about Camp Menominee, even though she'd refused to sit with them at the bonfire — "You guys don't want to go back, do you?"

"No!" they shouted.

River grinned and shrugged. "See?"

Molly had no idea what to say, or even what to think. She turned to her sister.

Dakota shrugged back. "I'd listen to Nature Boy, Mol. You're totally up to the task. This is your thing. Don't worry about me. You all have fun."

# X: S'more Romance

In theory, the rest of the afternoon and evening turned out perfectly.

Molly, River, and the ten campers arrived at the campsite earlier than expected. There weren't even that many mosquitoes. And the kids weren't only funny and cute, they were *helpful*. They helped put up the tents. They helped collect kindling for the fire. They helped with the cooking and cleaning: preparing the freeze-dried spaghetti, then washing the pots and pans in the nearby creek. Molly even found herself laughing as she and River chatted easily about how well they were behaving.

But after singing songs (River brought his guitar, of course), and roasting s'mores for dessert (River used a five-pronged twig), and telling the obligatory ghost story ("Camp Menominee was really founded by an evil madman who created a breed of vicious superintelligent owls, so beware!") . . . Molly felt a deep depression creep over her. It only worsened as she and River tucked their boy and girl campers in for bed, snug inside their respective tents. Yup. The night was *too* perfect. Or it wasn't. It was both and neither, because she knew now that as much fun as she and River were having, they would never get together. With a sigh, she sat back down by the fire.

Molly had forgotten how many stars you could see this far north. You could even see the ghostly tendril of the Milky Way. But she hadn't bothered to look much since she'd arrived. She was half-tempted to write about what else she'd forgotten she loved about camp, once she was sure her campers were asleep — but when she pulled the diary out of her backpack, she heard a rustling of the Eagle Cabin's tent flap.

"So what's up with that book my parents gave you?" River whispered, planting himself next to her. He reached for his guitar. "I remember when I bought that. It was at this yard sale in town. Dakota says you're using it as, like, a schedule?"

Molly snapped the book shut. Couldn't they go five minutes without talking about her sister? "No."

"Cool." River paused. "You know, I'm glad you decided to let Guido and Jess handle your sister's hike home. I love these overnights. I get cabin fever, crowded in with my guys every night." He began plucking at the strings.

"Yeah," Molly said tonelessly.

River took a deep breath. "What's up, Mol?" he asked.

Molly bit her lip. "Excuse me?"

"You've been acting weird to me ever since you got here!" His voice was agitated.

"I've been acting weird to *you*?" Molly couldn't decide whether she wanted to laugh or scream.

"Yes! You ignore me every single time you see me. What about at the bonfire last night? You didn't even sit with me!

165

And when Dakota hurt herself on the trail today, and I was trying to help her, you were all sour."

Molly raised her eyebrows. "All 'sour'? Hmm. First of all, Dakota was *clearly* faking. She didn't want to spend the night on some mountaintop — she wanted to go back and catch up on her beauty sleep. Get it?"

River twisted his lips. "She was faking?"

"Yeah, she was." Molly's voice rose. "She's a total Drama Queen! And, *F-Y-I*, you weren't trying to help her. You were hitting on her. Come on. You were stroking her leg in broad daylight!"

He gave a surprised cough. "Molly, that's ridiculous. I was checking to see —"

"How it felt. Yeah, I know. So tell me this: If you weren't hitting on her, then why did you make her a Summer Dish?" She bit her lip, her heart pounding. "I'm serious, River," she hissed, glancing back toward the tents to make sure none of their campers were stirring. "Why'd you do it?"

"What are you talking about?"

"Oh, come on," Molly groaned. "Don't play dumb."

He laughed, shaking his head. "Mol, I'm not the one who puts those names up —"

"Yeah, right!"

"I swear to you, I am *not* the one who puts The Summer Dishes on the menu."

Now it was Molly's turn to laugh. "You actually expect me to believe that?"

"You can believe whatever you want, but it's the truth. Anyway, why would I put a *guy's* name up?"

"So if it's not you, who is it, then?"

River blinked a few times and shook his head, a grin playing on his lips. "You wouldn't believe me if I told you."

"Clever answer," Molly snorted.

"It's my parents, Mol. My parents put up The Summer Dishes. Every year."

Molly rolled her eyes. "You're gonna have to do a little better than that, River. I was hoping you'd blame someone like Guido."

"I'm serious!" he cried, glancing toward his own campers' tent. "And you know what?" He lowered his voice and leaned close. "I've never told anyone that, except you. Every year, my mom and dad pick the two most spoiled and self-centered campers, put their names up on that chalkboard, and make it seem like some prankster did it. And every year, 'The Summer Dishes' end up *less* spoiled, because they get so much attention. They're on the spot all the time, so they actually find themselves having to be nice and help out. You know, the way they're supposed to. It's this . . . I don't know, this sixties reverse-psychology thing my parents are really into. But it works. I mean, look at Dakota."

"I've looked at her plenty," Molly muttered, not believing a word of what River was saying. "So have you."

River sighed. "Whatever. What I'm saying is, aside from wearing those sandals or whatever on the hike today, she's become a pretty decent CIT. Right?"

"Yup. She sure has. That's why you're gonna hook up with her. The way you always do with every hot new CIT who's a Summer Dish."

He brushed his dark hair out of his face. "Are you kidding?"

"River, every summer, you hook up with the girl on The Summer Dish menu!" Molly whispered. "Everybody sees you at the dance, and if you expect me to believe that your mom and dad —"

"I've never hooked up with any of them!" he interrupted. "I mean, my *parents* put their names up. I swear. It's weird — but none of them are ever my type, anyway." He paused. "Well . . . I know, I kissed Stacy Meyers three years ago, but that was an accident."

"Ha! An accident? Please."

River turned away sheepishly. "At the end of the dance, I went in for the hug, and she went in for the kiss. She didn't pull back. You know how it goes."

*I wish I did know,* Molly wanted to say. But she didn't.

River fell silent as well.

Molly stared at him. Was he telling the truth? Could it

possibly be that his parents were trying to teach Dakota a *lesson*? Her mind flashed back to Stacy Meyers . . . and now that she thought about it, Stacy had been just as blissfully clueless as Dakota. But she wasn't so bad, and she *had* gotten nicer. Molly could feel something bubbling inside her . . . maybe it was mostly exhaustion, a smoky whirlwind from how she was tired of lying, of keeping everything inside, of pulling back. At once, she realized River was staring at her. Molly, barely daring to believe what she was doing, leaned in close to River. He smelled of pine trees and wood smoke and suddenly he was leaning closer, too, and the stars seemed brighter and River Ween was kissing her. Or maybe Molly was kissing him. Their mouths fit together, their tongues touched, and Molly thought she might faint from happiness. *Please don't pull back*, she prayed silently, worried River might freak out and decide he was kissing the wrong sister.

But he only drew her closer, caressing her back, and she ran her hands through his soft hair — and she could feel the strength of his arms — but after what seemed either like a split second or an eternity, he drew away.

"Wait. Was *that* an accident?" Molly breathed.

"No. I don't think it was." He paused, his chest rising and falling quickly beneath his Camp Menominee T-shirt. "Do you?"

Molly shook her head. "I don't think so." She smiled.

He let out a deep sigh. "Good. Because, you know what?

I've been waiting six summers to do that. I've been waiting so long to kiss you, Mol, and to be honest, part of the reason I've danced with all those girls all those times was to make you jealous. I mean I know that sounds lame but —"

"Shh," she whispered, taking him into her arms again. "We don't want to wake the campers, you know?"

He smiled. "No, we don't."

Molly leaned close and kissed River again. And he didn't pull back for a long time. He didn't even try, and neither did she.


## XI: The Bombshell, Redux

Molly wasn't sure how to handle everything the next morning. She didn't want to act too differently. River seemed to feel similarly, though he did hold her hand during the hike back, when their campers weren't looking.

When she and the girls arrived at Sparrow Cabin just before noon, Molly was glowing — until she found Dakota and Jess snoring in their bunk bed, enjoying a day off. She supposed she should just be happy that Guido wasn't there.

"Dakota?" she said, clearing her throat.

Her little sister stretched and yawned. "Hey, Mol. Whaddup?"

"Oh, just another day of camp." Molly laughed. "Feel like being a CIT?"

Jess leaped out of the bottom bunk. "Oh, my God, jeez . . . Mol, I'm sorry." She rubbed her eyes. "Here, let me help. How about this? Mol, you check in with your sister, and you girls drop off your backpacks and sleeping bags, and I'll take everyone down to the lake for a swim. Looks like you could use a hosing down. . . . Sound good, girls?"

None of the girls even answered. They simply dropped their belongings, kicked off their boots, yanked off their socks, and started sprinting toward the lake — shrieking the entire way. Jess bolted after them. "Hey! Wait up! Don't you want to put on bathing suits? Skinny dipping is not allowed. . . ."

"Thanks, Jess!" Molly called with a sigh. She turned to her sister.

Dakota hopped down from the top bunk — landing bare-foot on her right ankle, without so much as a wince. She grinned. "So? How was the overnight? Anything fun happen? I don't need the super-juicy deets, just a yes or no."

Molly hesitated, chewing her lip. "Um —"

"I really hope so. I sort of planned the whole thing. I mean, I was hoping something would work out between you guys. It did, right?"

Molly blinked a few times. "Excuse me?"

"Between you and River, you know?"

171

"I . . . What are you saying? You planned . . . what?"

"Dude. I planned on getting you and River together! Well, Jess helped, I guess. You want to know the funny thing? She and I talked about setting something up between you guys the very first night. We hatched this, like, scheme to get you two alone. Or we hatched a plan to make a plan. We wanted to play Cupid. And Jess mentioned overnights, so . . ." Her voice trailed off.

The world spun beneath Molly's feet. "I'm sorry. *What* are you saying?"

"Well, ever since we got here, you've been so bummed out. And Jess and I started talking . . . and I had this realization. When Dark dumped me, I realized I at least knew what it was like to have an intense relationship. And that made me sad for you, because you've never had that. Especially cuz you're so much smarter than me —"

"I am not, Dakota," Molly protested. "You're really smart. I mean, you know movies and makeup and . . . lots of stuff."

Dakota smirked. "Don't try it, Mol. I'm a way better liar than you are. Let me finish. See, the thing is, the way Jess told it, I sort of figured out that you *did* have an intense relationship, only you didn't even know it. So I wanted — I don't know — I wanted to help you. You've always helped *me*. You know, with homework and chores and stuff. Plus, I wanted to take my mind off my own lame love life. I was also sort of wishing I'd meet some normal counselor up here, but I already knew that wasn't going to happen. I mean, Guido? And the rest of these boho types . . . well, you know."

Molly smiled, her eyes moistening. "Yeah, I do know. So what happens now?"

"Are you joking? Now I go home. I've never wanted to leave anywhere so badly in my life. River's mom is gonna drive me to the train station tonight. Anyway, you don't need a CIT. You've got Jess. Besides, my ankle is injured. And I can't deal with the bugs."

Molly managed a laugh. "Your ankle really is injured, huh?"

"Well, nah, I guess not so much. Just don't tell River's mom." Dakota laughed, too, then reached out and pulled Molly in for a quick hug. "Listen, I want you to have fun with River at the dance, okay?" she whispered. "And forget about The Summer Dishes. *You're* the Summer Dish. You know . . . IF you want to be."

"Thanks. That's sweet. I think I will just forget about it. Listen, Dakota, are you sure you don't want to stay? The campers love you."

"I love them, too, but honestly, I am having serious text withdrawal from my posse back home. Like, if I don't talk to Kylie or Amanda ASAP, I'm gonna —"

"I got it," Molly said drily. She stepped away.

Dakota's eyes twinkled. (It was amazing how pretty her sister's green eyes were without colored contacts.) "Thanks,

Mol," she said. "Hey, make sure you give the campers my cell number, okay? I already gave it to Jess. I want to stay in touch with everyone once they're outta here, too, so I can give them some pointers about the *real* world. And one more thing: Make sure the Weens don't play any, like, cheesy movie theme music at the dance. You know from, like, *You've Got Mail* or whatever? It would totally ruin the moment. I hate it when they do that."

## Epilogue: Song for The Summer Dishes

It would have been a dream had the song not stunk so badly.

Best just to focus on the good parts: her head nestled against River's chest as they swayed on the dance floor (aka the Rec Hall, with a cheap little disco ball strung up from the ceiling for "effect," compliments of the Weens). With her arms draped around his waist, breathing in the scent of pine on his neck . . . she was doing what she'd envisioned for six years. Finally. Molly Walker was snuggled up to River Ween as a lame slow jam blasted at the dance. Who even *sang* this song? Kevin Federline? Whatever. It didn't matter. It was tradition. This was what the summer before college was *supposed* to be.

She sighed, her heart fluttering, and pulled River closer. Out of the corner of her eye, she caught a quick glimpse of

Jess and Guido, clinging to each other at the opposite end of the room. Jess's gaze met hers, and she smiled and flashed a quick thumbs-up. So she'd finally decided to take the Guido plunge — on the last night of camp. Good for her.

Too bad Dakota wasn't here to witness it.

"What are you thinking?" River breathed, stroking her hair.

"That I miss my sister," Molly said. "And also, that this is the worst song ever!"

*SCREECH!*

Molly winced. She giggled once, plugging her ears, and stepped away from River, who frowned at his mom and dad. In addition to trying to lend the Rec Hall a cheesy seventies vibe, the Weens also insisted on being DJs, using a freakish amalgam of an old boom box, a turntable, and a CD player — all wired into an ancient electric guitar amplifier that Mr. Ween had used when he'd dreamed of being a rock star, probably before he was River's age.

Everyone stared.

"Sorry about that!" Mr. Ween yelled. "I hate to interrupt, campers, but I have a special announcement. It's a song request. And it's coming across several state lines. It's from our erstwhile Summer Dish, Dakota Walker. She wrote us a letter, if you can believe it. And she asked me to say the following: *FYI: No crap songs at the dance. I want my . . .*" He hesitated for a moment, his eyes narrowing at the slip of paper.

175

"I want my 'peeps' to have a good time. This will do it for them." He shrugged. "Well, let's hear it for Dakota Walker! We miss her!"

Molly clapped her hands and hooted. She clapped and hooted louder than any other camper.

With that, Mr. Ween dropped the needle on the record. A lilting synthesized drumbeat thumped from the speaker. It was a beat that Molly recognized in an instant, and one that sent a shiver of delight down her spine.

River's face crinkled. "Ugh. What is this? It's so old school. And not in a good way."

Molly had to smile. "Not in a good way? Are you kidding? It's called: 'Ain't It Good to Be a Gangsta.' I think we should make it our song."

River grinned and swept her back in his arms. "Whatever you say, Mol. Whatever you say."

★　★　★　★　★　★　★

# NIGHT
# SWIMMING

## By Niki Burnham

★　★　★　★　★　★　★

# One

Here's the big secret of my life: I, Wynn Michaela O'Malley, despise summer.

Not that I despise summer itself — I'd really have to be a bitch and a half to hate summer. I love that everyone is in a good mood, that school's out, and that there are flowers in pots on the sidewalks all over town. It's more that I hate what happens to me in the summer.

Through no fault of my own, I appear ugly and antisocial.

Note, I said *appear*. I'm not *actually* ugly or antisocial. I don't need to go talk to a therapist or school counselor about my low self-esteem or anything. I wish that were the problem, but no. I have solid reasons for thinking summer stinks.

First, and the reason that trumps all the others, is that I'm pale. Not any ordinary pale, either. Yeah, I have the platinum blond hair and blue eyes thing people conjure up in their heads when they hear the word *pale*. However, when I say I'm pale, I mean I'm pale as in way, way white. Kindergarten paste, Rembrandt smile, and darned close to glow-in-the-dark white.

The other girls I know — every one of them — look much better than I do in a swimsuit, because even if they are on the paler end of the skin-tone spectrum, and even if we have the exact same body type, by mid-June they all have that summery golden glow guys love. The kind of glow that gives the illusion that they're thinner than they really are and that their skin is butter-soft. That they're natural athletes with muscle tone and not a care in the world.

Naturally I feel like a butt-ugly, unathletic, and uninteresting person in comparison. Like I'm ill and just got released from a long stint in a windowless hospital. Now, I don't feel that way at all when I'm hanging out with friends *indoors*. Like, at school or when we drive to Alexandria to catch a movie at the Midway Mall. It's more an out-at-the-lake, in-the-bright-sunshine thing.

Second, my friends don't seem to grasp why I might not want to spend every freakin' second outdoors during the summer. They argue that I must have some other reason for not wanting to be outside with them, like maybe I'm keeping some deep dark secret. Joking back with, "I'm sorry, but I simply lack the required amount of melanin" doesn't resonate with them. They're certain it's that I don't like them anymore.

Third, nearly all the decent summer jobs around where we live in central Minnesota are outdoors (landscaping, lifeguarding, that kind of thing) and since I can't convince the owner of the local paper to hire me, I'm stuck every summer making minimum wage at the Dairy Darling, with the evil owner Raymond telling me not to make the scoops so big. (Who goes into the ice-cream business if they're a total Scrooge? Ice cream is all about *happy*. Especially if it's mint chocolate chip. I give extra-big scoops of that, particularly to little kids. Well, I give little kids extra-big scoops of all the flavors.) Needless to say, having to spend forty hours a week with Mean Raymond glaring at me puts me in a less-than-stellar mood.

Therefore, because people's perceptions of my attractiveness and my friendliness drop as the thermometer rises, I've developed an aversion to summer.

But this year, instead of spending my summer doling out too-small scoops or trying to enjoy the fresh air and sunshine from a protected area under a big, striped canopy, I have a plan. A plan to avoid the downsides of summer, while simultaneously giving my friends the impression that I'm my normal, friendly, not-unattractive self.

I'm taking a cue from Nicole Kidman.

Ever wonder why the tabloids don't run pics of Nicole Kidman lying out on the beach in a bikini? It's certainly not because she's ugly. It's because she knows that sitting out in the sun in all her colorless glory will make her look really, really bad in photographs and possibly harm her career (much in the way it harms my social life). So she doesn't set herself up for that.

Because she's an Aussie, she has the option of traveling between beautiful houses in the States and in Australia. Both are sunny places, but they have summer at opposite times of the year. She can go to Australia in the winter, where she's not going to fry every time she goes outside, then come back to California when it's summer in Oz . . . and do winter again!

It's brilliant, really.

I don't have a fantastic house in Australia. The house my family has in Minnesota isn't even all that great. It's a split-level built in the mid-'60s and has a roof that needs to be replaced. But I think Nicole has the right idea.

You just have to run away from summer.

While I can't go to Australia, I *can* do what I normally do when it's winter. Go to school.

Insane, I know. But when I told my friends that I was web-surfing and found this great program at a private college in Delaware that allows kids between their junior and senior years in high school to stay in the dorms and take a class for college credit — you can choose classes like Creative Writing, Astronomy, Anthropology, or Environmental Economics — they thought it sounded cool. Not like real school, but like I might be going away, meeting new people, having an *adventure*. Getting to *write*, which is the thing I want to do most in the world (so *pffft* on the newspaper owner for not hiring me.) And, as I explained to my friends, it's only one class a day, so it's not like I'm stuck at a desk all the time. The program also includes weekend and evening excursions — evening being key for me — where students can go horseback riding or hiking in nearby state parks.

Needless to say, my parents were all over it.

Mom and Dad totally sympathize with my hatred of the Dairy Darling — and, more specifically, of Mean Raymond — so when I raised the subject of possibly going to Delaware and earning a few college credits during summer vacation, they responded with enthusiasm, using phrases like "unique opportunity" and "broadening horizons," and helped me get my application together and mailed out in less than a week.

My adrenaline levels went into overdrive and I think I danced around the house for a solid month after I got the acceptance letter and a thick information packet, complete with pictures of the brick, four-story dorm. (Sweet!)

I might've danced through the airport when I landed. I dunno. I was too excited by the fact that I was in DELAWARE! And that right at the curb waiting for me was a van headed for Wriston College, which I am positive is a good place to meet guys. Gorgeous, intelligent, *college* guys. Guys who are more interested in my brain than in how good I look while preening lakeside.

Unfortunately now that I've been in my dorm room a whopping five minutes and I'm looking out the window, past the parking lot where a half dozen people — including some *very* cute guys — are unloading their stuff from the back of another airport van, I discover that I've screwed up.

Big-time.

183

# Two

I take a deep breath, try to get a Zen vibe going, and tell myself that this doesn't matter. I am still going to meet tons of fabulous people, take a class I would never get to take back at my high school, and see things I never would have seen otherwise.

I am still going to be living like a grown-up, without having to ask my parents' permission before leaving the house or explaining to them that I'll be just fine if I stay up late or want an extra serving of ice cream.

I tell myself that *it's all good*.

Delaware, as it turns out, is on the beach. Or, I should say, the part of Delaware where Wriston College is located is beachfront property. I know because said beachfront is right there, out my window. Didn't see it on the way in — the road from the airport entered campus from the other direction — but from the third floor of my dorm, Dixon Hall, it's clearly visible. And very close.

On the positive side, I have to admit that I am loving this view. It's not one of those kind of beaches with volleyball players or bikini-clad sunbathers you see actresses frequenting in *Us Weekly*. Instead, it's that pristine, sandy, walkable kind of beach you see in Calvin Klein and Ralph Lauren ads — the ones filmed in black and white, usually with a Kate Moss type wearing unwrinkled linen and moving in slow motion with her hair flowing out behind her, looking over her shoulder at an unseen person who's making her laugh.

There's no one walking around in linen, but as my gaze travels along the length of a dock, I notice that a bunch of people are sitting on the end in long shorts and T-shirts, dangling their feet over the surface of the water and laughing in a very Calvin Klein–like way. Like there's nothing more important in the world than whatever they're discussing at the end of that dock.

In Minnesota, I look out my bedroom window at trees, trees, trees. Snow in the winter, mosquitoes the size of walnuts in the summer. It's a twenty-minute drive to the lake, and the sand there was brought in by heavy machinery and dumped onto the shore. So this is a nice change.

But how did it not occur to me that Delaware is freaking *coastal*? I mean, I know Delaware is on the East Coast (duh), and if I'd thought about it for two seconds, I'd have told anyone that yes, of course, Delaware has beaches. They even have a lighthouse on the web site for Wriston College. But when I was reading the web pages outlining the benefits of Creative Writing 102, I didn't think about surf, bright sun, or the phrase *heat index*.

I thought about how I was escaping another summer of ostracism. How I was going to do something *fun* — because I am happiest when I can sit back with a gel pen and notebook and just write — while I got to meet a whole new group of people from all over the country.

Telling myself (again) to make the best of it — because really, I'm still going to get to spend my summer writing, and the proximity of sand doesn't change anything — I reach up to crank open the window. Now I know why the air felt so strange and fabulous when I got out of the airport van and walked into the dorm. Even if I can't enjoy the beach up close and personal during the warmest part of the day, at least I can enjoy the non-Minnesota smell of it. Or, if my roomie turns out to be the type who doesn't mind, maybe we can sleep with the window open and hear it.

The crank on the window doesn't want to work. I pull it harder, but it won't give.

"There's a flipper thing at the bottom. You have to do that first," a male voice says behind me.

I turn around to see a guy my age with sun-lightened brown hair leaning against the frame of my open door. He's wearing a pair of long khaki shorts, a white T-shirt with big red letters that shout BAMA!, and a pair of Teva sandals that look to have a lot of miles on them. One side of his mouth hitches up in that expression guys make when they're about to give you a half-assed apology. "Sorry if I'm, like, intruding or something —"

"It's all right —"

"— but I was walking by and saw you yankin' the crank and figured I'd let you know. It took me a while to figure it out."

186

I manage not to crack up at the way the guy says *yankin'
the crank*. You'd think, with an Alabama shirt, that he'd sound
Southern, but he doesn't. Not quite.

I turn back toward the window, locate a lever near the bottom, and push it out. There's a light popping sound as the crank
loosens so I can open the windows. I spin it, then look back
toward the BAMA! guy. "Thanks. I'd have probably broken it."

He nods, then takes a step backward into the hall, like he
thinks he's invaded my personal space.

"I'm Wynn."

He grins and eases back into my room. "Caleb."

Yeah, he looks like a Caleb. Relaxed. Honest. *Wise*. That's
the strongest impression I get.

He does the whole nice-to-meet-you thing, then says he's
in the summer program, too. His room's on the floor above
mine, but he came down here because the water fountain on
his floor's broken. "Last day of school was chaotic, I guess. It
got smashed."

This dorm is gorgeous, and the brochure says it's one of
the most prestigious and hard to get into on campus during the
regular school year. I couldn't imagine having the urge to
smash anything. I mean, do college kids always get that crazy
after finishing their finals? How stupid is that?

"I know," he says, as if I'd uttered the thought aloud, "I
can't imagine wanting to smash a water fountain, just 'cause
school's done for the year."

He tells me he'll leave me alone so I can unpack, and I thank him for the window advice. It's one of those times where you feel kind of silly, like you know you could talk to this person and be good friends because there's this vibe of understanding between you. But since you just met, you don't want to look like you're desperate for a friend by asking them to come in and sit on the bed, because then you end up talking about something idiotic like what they watched on TV last night or how they enjoyed their flight.

"There's no dinner in the dorm tonight," he says. "My roommate and I are ordering pizza. You can come up if you want. Around six or so. Room 454."

I tell him I might do that, even though I'm afraid I'll chicken out. Seeing the beach out my window — as beautiful as it is — has knocked a bit of the confidence out of me.

He slides his hands into his back pockets, gives me a see-ya-later, then walks out.

I am so *freaking* stupid.

I should have told him he could come in and hang out. Asked where his roommate is from and how he likes him. I might've found out if he signed up for Creative Writing or if he's going to be in another class.

I hate that I think of these things the minute it's too late to say any of them.

"Hey! You must be Lynn!"

A girl with streaky brown hair, freckles, and a huge smile

188

pops in the door. She makes a show of arching her back to look at the number over the door. "I'm Kelly. If this is room 358, then I'm your roomie!"

She's pulling a purple suitcase behind her that's bigger than any I've seen in my life. She's not tall — I'd guess not even five feet — but she whips the thing inside and lifts it onto the empty bed as if it were the weight of cotton candy.

"Thanks for giving me the bed by the door. I've always gotta pee in the middle of the night," she says. "Which closet is mine? I wanna get unpacked and hit the beach. Isn't it *fantastic*?"

"I, um. . . ." How'd she (sort of) know my name?

Kelly keeps talking as she unzips her suitcase. "There was a guy in the hall who said 358 was down here, and that I must be Lynn's roommate. Smokin' hot guy, I must say, but I want beach more than boy right now. It's unbelievable. I had no clue we were gonna be so close! The piles of papers they sent me didn't advertise *that*. Probably because they figure they'll get a lot of partiers applying instead of people who want to" — she drops her voice an octave — "immerse themselves in a program of stimulating academics in a safe, precollege environment."

"Yeah, it surprised me too." I can't believe I got a word in. Her energy level is throwing me off. She also nailed the language from the web site, which is rather disturbing.

I tell her to take whichever closet, that I haven't picked

one yet and really don't care which one I get. Then I say, "Oh, and my name's Wynn. With a W. Not Lynn. But no biggie — a lot of people get it wrong."

"Wynn?" She has her back to me, shoving stuff into the closet as if moving into a dorm is an everyday thing for her. "Like, short for Winifred or something?"

"Nope, just Wynn."

She spins around to grab another stack of clothes from the open suitcase on her bed. "Whew. I was afraid I was gonna have to keep it secret all summer that I hate the name Winifred. I have an aunt named Winifred, and she's, like, practically mummified she's so stiff and old. But Wynn's cool. Kinda like winner. Really positive energy to it, ya know?"

I shrug. I mean, what can I say to all that? She does seem pretty nice, so I think that even with her super-talky, hyper streak, I'm going to be okay. Maybe she'll even be good for me. There's no way someone like her isn't going to attract a ton of people — male and female — to our room, so I'm bound to make a lot of new friends without having to put myself out there too much.

I hate when my parents tell me I need to "put myself out there."

"Screw it," Kelly mutters, whipping the closet door closed. She rummages through the stack of clothes still in her suit-case, fishes out a bright yellow halter bikini, and starts to strip.

She's kicked her jeans into the closet and has her panties off before I process that the door is wide open.

I can't believe this chick has her naked bum right there for anyone walking by to see. And she *knows* that the guys come down here since she ran into Caleb in the hallway.

I have no desire to become known as the *Girls Gone Wild* room.

"Um, lemme get that," I say, walking toward the door.

"No prob, I'm quick." And she is. She's got her bikini bottom on before I can grab the door handle. Still, I close it while she gets her top on.

And here I was nervous about changing clothes in front of a roommate. I mean, I change in the locker room at school before volleyball practice and gym class, but this is different. At least it *feels* different. Maybe because I've known the girls at school since I was old enough to go on playdates. And we're all pretty discreet about how we change. We keep the locker doors open and stand between them, towels held strategically so we don't flash anyone.

Kelly grabs a big towel out of her suitcase, then throws a bottle of sunscreen and a pair of shades into a backpack that looks like it's meant for classes more than for the beach.

"You wanna come?"

"Nah, think I'll unpack." But she sure makes me want to go. I might risk a sunburn just to see what she'll do next.

Well, I would if I'd packed a swimsuit. Didn't occur to me — I was too worried about how to pack eight weeks' worth of clothes into one suitcase, get it on the plane, and find my way here without my parents flipping out about me traveling alone.

Which reminds me . . .

"Also, I need to call my parents and let them know I made it."

"Ah, crap. Me too." She makes a face, then scrambles to find her purse. "I came from Orlando. My parents freaked about me flying up here by myself. Don't know why. I mean, the van friggin' met us at the airport and drove us here. Where could I possibly have gotten lost? And it's not like I didn't spend every summer away at camp when I was a kid. I'll call 'em from the beach." She pulls her cell phone and a few dollars from her purse, tosses them into the backpack with her room key, then yells a "Ciao!" before disappearing out the door.

When she's not back four hours later, I decide it's a good thing I didn't go with her. In the meantime, I've managed to unpack, let my parents know that my plane didn't crash, walk around campus so I could find the bookstore and student union (Dad's suggestion), then get back and change into my fave turquoise Gap skirt and white Express halter top.

Now I'm standing in front of a door on the fourth floor, wondering what'll happen now that I've knocked, assuming anyone can hear me in there. It's loud enough to be a party.

I wonder if I can make it down the hall and back to my room before anyone notices?

A reedy, chocolate-skinned guy with thick glasses gives me a "Hey!" as he opens the door. Definitely no chance to run now.

"Hi. This is Caleb's room, I hope?" It comes out sounding all nervous and goofy. Or, as my Mom says, like my Minnesota is showing.

"Yup. I'm his roommate, Cortez." He pushes the door the rest of the way open and waves me in. There's all kinds of activity going on behind him, and from what I'm picking up of the conversation, it involves a drill. "You Wynn?"

I nod, trying not to look surprised. So it was Kelly who screwed up my name, not Caleb. And Caleb must've told Cortez to expect me. "What are they doing?"

He rolls his eyes and he waves me to the opposite side of the room. He takes a seat on a battered brown couch with a thick wooden frame. I sit a good arm's length away, making sure there's space for a third person, but still close enough to Cortez to be friendly-casual.

"Caleb found this sofa outside," Cortez explains. "Someone who graduated last week dumped it there, and Caleb figured we could fit it in our room if we made bunk beds out of our twins. It was a bitch getting it up the stairs, but I think it'll be worth it."

Looking at what's going on in front of me, I'm not so sure.

Caleb is hunched over between the wall and the lower bed, looking for something on the floor, while two other guys are holding the top bunk in place. A girl with red hair and model-perfect bone structure is standing next to them, wrestling a bent extension cord plug into a wall socket. When she finishes, she gives a huge smile and a thumbs-up to Caleb, who I now notice is holding a drill and has found a drill bit he apparently dropped on the floor.

"Are the beds made to do that?" I ask Cortez in between surges from the drill.

Cortez looks doubtful. "Caleb says the RA — the resident assistant — told him that they're designed to be separate or hooked up as bunks. He showed Caleb how to do it. Theoretically."

Cortez and I sit on the sofa while the rest of the group assemble the bed. There's some arguing over which size bit Caleb should be using, but it seems to go okay and, eventually, they get the top bunk mounted over the lower one.

Not sure I'd trust the bed enough to sleep on it, so I hope Caleb and Cortez will be all right.

"Pizza's on the way," Cortez says while everyone else tosses pillows and bedding up to the top bunk. "I hooked up my Xbox before they started the construction project. You wanna play a game? I've got *Ridge Racer*, *Perfect Dark* —"

"You promised me first turn!" The redheaded girl who

plugged in the extension cord picks up a controller from the window ledge.

I tell the girl and Cortez to go ahead. I've only played on an Xbox a couple of times, so I think I'm better off watching a couple games. Once they start — a football game that looks very lifelike and very complicated — I'm pretty much forgotten. But that's okay. It's giving me a chance to watch Caleb (discreetly, of course) while he stands on the frame of the lower bunk and makes the top bunk.

He's surprisingly good at making a bed. Tight corners, pillows just so. Yet there's something in his body language that makes it appear casual. Like if you could only see him, not the bed, you'd guess from his actions that there'd be lumps and sticky-out places.

A few more people show up, and just behind them is the pizza guy. Caleb collects money from everyone, Cortez pauses the game, and then it's a free-for-all with the pizza. I grab a slice and go to the end of the couch. As I eat, I watch how everyone else interacts. They all seem like they've known each other for years, even though I have to assume they all met today. I nod along when someone makes a comment, laugh at the appropriate times, but don't talk much. I wonder how many of them have done programs like this before. I wonder how good their grades are, or if they're popular back at their own high schools.

I bet Cortez is way popular. He seems to know that people listen to him, even when he's speaking quietly. The red-head — who seems to be attracting a lot of attention — strikes me as the popular type too. It'll be interesting to see if the two of them end up being popular here at Wriston.

I'm trying to guess whether either of them might have a significant other back home when I realize Caleb's looking at me. His eyes are smiling as he passes me a second piece of pizza. Even though I didn't ask for it, he seems to know I want it.

And suddenly I realize that I could be madly attracted to this guy. I can't put my finger on exactly why — it's just a gut thing — but it unnerves me.

"Which class you register for?" he asks.

"Creative Writing. How about you?"

I'm expecting Anthropology. Maybe Astronomy or Environmental Economics. But he says, "Same. Cool."

I take a bite of the slice he handed me and make an *uh-hunh* sound. I want to say something witty, something to let him know I am glad but not girly-ecstatic about him being in my class. But by the time I swallow, he's turned away, laughing at Cortez and the redheaded girl's tug-of-war over a breadstick. I keep right on smiling and eating my pizza.

I suspect I won't be one of the popular people.

# Three

If I were to play a word association game — you know, the kind where someone says "stoplight" and someone else replies with "red" because it's the first thing that pops into her mind — I would have said "dorms" or "tough" or maybe even "expensive" if someone zinged me with "college."

I would not have said "beach."

Twenty minutes into our first class, though, Professor Conroy (who tells us to call her Nina, which does feel more appropriate for a woman with a pixie cut who's wearing a broomstick skirt and has multiple piercings) says that an important component of writing fiction is to learn how to let the words flow onto the page without engaging our internal editor. In other words, she believes that the best stories happen when we stop worrying about where to put the commas or about what a teacher or a friend will think about what we're writing, and we give ourselves permission to blurp everything out onto the page.

That was her word. *Blurp.*

She tells us we'll learn to clean up the blurp later.

To me, it sounds like someone's been sick all over a bathroom and left the mopping to others.

In order to do this, she wants us to go to the beach. The beach, she claims, is a place where our brains naturally relax, and that it's important to find triggers — she calls them *anchors* — to help us get our brains to that relaxed place in order to write.

First, however, she wants us to go around the room and introduce ourselves by our full names (why?!), say where we're from, and give one interesting tidbit about where we live.

Nina starts with the redhead — the only person other than Caleb that I recognize from pizza the night before — who introduces herself as Bayleigh Lynn Hart. Bayleigh says she lives in Edgartown on Martha's Vineyard year-round. Since I don't know anyone who actually specifies "year-round" when they say where they're from, and everyone *ooohs* when she says it, I get the feeling it must be a really cool place. For her tidbit, she says that her basketball team has to take a ferry whenever they play away games.

Everyone seems impressed. I know I am.

After a few more people, I'm up. I introduce myself, say I'm from Alexandria (because it's the closest town of any size to my house and I don't want to sound too rural by saying Dawson, which has a population of just over a hundred). For my tidbit, I say that most people in my town work for 3M, the company that makes everything from Scotchlite — the reflective material used on safety vests and firefighters' gear — to Post-It Notes and packing tape.

No one looks overly impressed, but it does draw a few positive laughs, which helps me relax a little.

When it's finally Caleb's turn, he introduces himself — his middle name turns out to be Wilson — and says he lives in Fort Rucker, Alabama. He turns to look at Nina, since he was the last one, but she reminds him that he is supposed to share a tidbit. I can tell from his expression that he didn't want to come up with one. After a couple seconds, he says, "There are a lot of helicopters in Fort Rucker. Lots of guys running around with Scotchlite, too."

This cracks everyone up.

"I'm going to give you fifteen minutes," Nina says. "Go back to your rooms, grab a bottle of water and a hat, then meet me in the Dixon Hall lobby. Don't forget your notepads and pens! We'll extend class by fifteen minutes today to make up the time, so if you're late, you can expect class to be extended further. Understood?"

It's only a three-minute walk from the classroom to our dorm, so fifteen minutes later, I'm in the lobby of Dixon Hall, coated head to toe in sunscreen and carrying more in my backpack. I've changed into a lighter-weight shirt, but nearly everyone else has changed into swimwear — baggy swim shorts on the guys, bikinis with T-shirts or flippy skirts (never both) on the girls. Even Caleb is in flip-flops and swim trunks, no shirt.

I try not to look. Well, I try not to be *obvious* about looking. Caleb without a shirt is a sight to behold. He's tan, which makes his abs look lean and tight, but not overly so. Not like a guy who lives in the gym for the sole purpose of scoring with girls by flaunting his six-pack.

He's leaning against the wall on the opposite side of the lobby from me, next to a bank of metal mailboxes, chatting with a guy who introduced himself in class as Marc from Quebec City and said that most of his friends speak French at home. I can't for the life of me remember his middle or last names. He and Caleb look like they're going to be good friends.

As I watch, it hits me that even shirtless, Caleb's relaxed and comfortable, like it doesn't occur to him that anyone would be checking him out, when in reality everyone is checking out everyone else because it's the first day of class and now we're (almost) all in swimsuits.

Nina walks into the lobby, dressed just as she was before. She doesn't seem to notice that all the students changed clothes. Or maybe she was expecting it. She counts heads, reminds us that this is class and not social hour and we'll be expected to work when we get to the beach, then she leads us out of the dorm and along the beach path. Once our feet hit the sand, she tells us to spread out and write about our impressions of the water, the rocks, or whatever captures our attention.

"This isn't for a grade," she emphasizes. "We'll deal with that type of assignment later. Today is all about tapping into your creative self. Learning to let go and to just lay all your emotions onto the page. Just let the words roll from your pen, even if you think what you're writing is stupid or it doesn't make sense when read aloud. It's the first step to everything we'll learn this summer. *Blurp* it out. Got it?"

We all nod, then pick our spots on the beach. I manage to find a place where I'm semi-protected from the sun, with my back against a narrow wooden shack meant for changing clothes (but that's far enough from the beach's parking lot that I doubt it gets much use) then pull out my notebook. Even I have to admit it's gorgeous out — the sky is liquid blue, the clouds are as light as froth on a cappuccino — but it's blazing hot. There's a slight breeze, but it's just enough to ruffle the pages of my notebook without actually cooling me off.

I pull out my pen, open my just-purchased notebook to the first page, then let the pen tip rest against the page while I think about what to write.

Nothing happens.

There's no creative anything happening with me. All I can produce is a trickle of sweat that runs next to my eye, mixing with sunscreen before I swipe it away.

I glance around discreetly, so Nina thinks I'm working, and notice that all the other people in my class are writing furiously. Pretty much all the girls are lying on towels in their bikinis, some with sunglasses on, others with ponytails carefully looped through the backs of baseball hats, the brims shading their eyes. A few of the guys — including Quebec

City Marc — have walked to the dock and are writing with their notebooks in their laps, feet hanging over the edge.

I scan the beach for Caleb, but I don't see him. There's a big gray rock right where the water is rolling up on the sand, obscuring my view of the people who went that direction. Bummer. He'd have been interesting to watch.

I glance down at my blank paper. A blue splotch the size of a dime has formed where the tip of my pen leaked ink.

I wonder what Caleb is writing about?

I typically wouldn't have trouble getting started on this kind of assignment — writing has always come easily to me — but I feel self-conscious in the heat and my state of (comparative) overdress and the words won't come. I outline the ink circle, then stare at it.

I feel Nina's gaze on me, so for the next hour, I doodle. I make bigger and bigger circles around the ink splotch, and I get so into it, drawing pictures of spirals, hot-air balloons, airplanes, and archery targets, that when I hear Nina walking around and announcing that class is over and she'll see us tomorrow, I stare at my page of bad art and freak.

I sure hope she means it when she says this won't be graded.

When I get back to my room, Kelly's already there. She's hunched over her desk, staring at the screen on her laptop, talking to herself.

"Hey, how was Environmental Economics?" I ask. Gotta be better than my non-writing session.

"Suck City, Señorita Wynn-ita." She leans back and jams her fingers into her hair. "This class is gonna involve some serious homework. We have a ton of reading already, plus the math is all, like, the toughest stuff I've ever done. I think I can handle it, but it's gonna blow out my brain cells. How 'bout you?"

I give a brief explanation of blurping. She tells me I got off easy compared to her. "Bet you get some huge writing assignments soon to make up for it. And don't believe the professors when they tell you something's not graded. They're still gonna wanna look at it, and it's like they" — she puts her fingers to her temples and makes a spinning motion — "like they get these expectations in their brains based on so-called non-graded stuff, judging you based on what they think you produce when you're not trying. They pigeonhole you."

I'm not sure how she knows all this, but she sounds certain.

We go to lunch together, where we sit with a group of people from her Environmental Economics class. They talk about how stressful they think their class is going to be. I keep my mouth shut about Creative Writing. I doubt the economics types would get Nina's methods — especially since they all call their professor by his last name and he snarls at them if they forget the "professor" part and say "mister" like we do at high school. Instead, I look around the room, taking in the food line, the milk and juice dispensers, and the tables full of students, all of whom are part of the summer program.

A few tables away, I see a group of kids from Creative Writing. Caleb's at the end, with Bayleigh next to him. She says something, then puts her hand on his arm and starts laughing her head off. A few other kids are laughing, too. Caleb's smiling at her. It makes me wonder what she said.

I take a long sip of my milk and decide that eating in a college dorm isn't any different than eating in my high school cafeteria. Well, aside from the fact that Kelly, who's sitting beside me, has more energy than any ten people I know at my high school (yes, color me jealous). The dorm cafeteria is bigger, but there are twice as many people in the summer program as in my entire middle-of-nowhere high school, so that's no surprise. What's odd is that the conversations are the same, the food is similar, and the feel of the whole meal is the same. People are half thinking about their classes and half thinking about what the people around them are thinking.

Somehow, I thought the whole college experience would be more . . . I dunno. . . . Different.

At ten P.M., long after Kelly has crashed (I think yesterday's travel and beach excursion finally caught up with her) I lie awake in bed, fidgeting in discomfort. First, because I'm used to sleeping in a queen, and this is a twin. Second, because the sheets, which the dorm provides to us for the summer, don't smell like the sheets at home. Third, because I'm thinking about Kelly's statement that Nina is going to mentally grade the work she claims isn't being graded, comparing my writing skills to the rest of the class. And finally, because the window is open and the night air and the sounds are so different than at home.

And they're calling to me.

I whisper Kelly's name, then try it a little louder. She doesn't answer. I get up, scribble a note, and pull on a pair of shorts. I grab my notebook and the emergency flashlight Mom made me put in my suitcase (she was convinced the dorm would catch fire and I'd need it to get out) and head downstairs.

I have to get something on paper other than doodles.

No one's in the halls as I make my way to the staircase, though I hear voices behind some of the doors; roommates are laughing and getting to know one another or working late on homework to impress their professors.

I make it to the beach in five minutes. I can hear the sounds from the parking lot and I see a couple of girls who've been out walking at the edge of the surf making their way back toward the dorms. Otherwise, I have the whole place to myself.

Once I'm past the rocks, I kick off my flip-flops and carry them while I let my toes squish in the sand. I find a place near the big gray rock and plunk myself down. The tide is coming

205

in, so I won't be able to stay here long, but it's peaceful. Just the lull of the surf, the occasional sound of a far-off car engine.

I get the same peaceful feeling I have in my bedroom at home when I open up the window and listen to the sounds of the insects in the trees and the *swish-swash* of the dishwasher running in the kitchen right below me.

And I write.

# Four

Eight pages. I can hardly believe it.

When I wake up in the morning, I glance over what I wrote by flashlight at the beach and count, just to be sure. I don't think I've ever written eight pages straight before. I definitely blurped, as Nina would say. I didn't edit at all as I went along, but it's still pretty good. All about my home in Dawson, Minnesota, and about the lakes and barbecues and the Dairy Darling. About driving to Alexandria when I need things from the mall or when I visit Dad in his office and steal Jelly Bellies from the jar on his assistant's desk and feel like I'm part of the crowd there.

Nothing anyone else would care about, but little aspects of my life that I treasure.

I slide the notebook into my backpack and head to class.

The minute Nina gets to the front of the room, she asks us to take out what we wrote yesterday. I expect her to talk about anchors, or maybe about how to edit what we wrote yesterday, but no.

She wants it handed in.

A rumble of protest goes through the room and a couple people start scribbling fast. Including Caleb.

"No, no, no," she says, waving her hands. She's wearing a lot of rings. "Don't start writing now. Get those papers to the front. I told you yesterday, it's not graded. It's just an exercise."

In a room of overachievers, this still doesn't go over well. Nina gathers all the papers, then walks to the corner near the door to stick them in a worn leather briefcase. She pauses just as she's about to slide them in, then pulls one off the top and frowns.

"Marc Bouchard?"

A grunt comes from a few rows behind me.

"Only one page? In an hour and a half? Next time, I think you can do better."

He mumbles an okay, and she shoves his paper to the bottom of the stack. Her eyes open wide at the next paper.

"And Caleb Rowles?"

His hand goes up in a halfhearted wave. He's sitting two rows over from me and one seat up. And he doesn't look happy.

"The point of this exercise was to blurp. No editing, no

contemplation. To just emote on paper and scrawl anything — anything at all — that came to your mind."

He doesn't respond.

She addresses the whole class. "I'm sure many of you understood the assignment, given the thickness of the stack of papers that were handed in. But in ninety minutes, I definitely expect more than a paragraph. And you knew it, too, didn't you, Caleb? It's apparent you tried to add an extra paragraph this morning with that blue pen that's in your hand." She gestures toward him, and he doesn't try to hide the blue Paper Mate. "The first paragraph here is in black; the handwriting's neat. This second is scribbled. Just because I told you it wasn't for a grade doesn't mean you shouldn't make an effort."

She holds up the paper and clears her throat. My stomach sinks for Caleb. How could she do this?

*"Why would someone be nervous about eating pizza? Not the pizza part, but the idea of 'let's all order pizza and hang out.' I want to know that kind of person better and find out why she's too timid (or edgy?) to talk."*

The room is silent. I think I'm gonna yack.

Is he talking about me, or Bayleigh?

It's got to be me, I realize. Bayleigh was talking the whole time I was up there. She wasn't nervous at all.

*He wrote about me?*

I'm too petrified to look around, so I do a mental census of the room — other than Bayleigh, were any other students from this class in the group that had pizza? Hopefully, Bayleigh was so busy playing Xbox or fighting Cortez for the breadstick that she didn't really notice I was there.

Maybe.

Nina looks all around the room, catching each person's eye, and then continues, "That's all you had on the page. Then this morning, in the blue pen, you write, *'How can someone spend over an hour on the beach and write nothing, yet staple together a bunch of pages the next day? I'm very curious.'*"

This is definitely about me.

"I don't read this to embarrass you, but to make a point," Nina continues. "Caleb — and everyone else — this is not blurping. It's very conscious writing. A lot of thought went into it before your pen went on the page yesterday. While I do like what you have here — it's good stuff, quite intriguing — we're trying to get away from conscious writing with this assignment."

For the rest of class, I can hardly think. Nina talks about tapping into our inner well. . . . I guess. My mind keeps drifting to Caleb and what he wrote. And the fact that Nina's sure he put thought into it before writing it.

When the clock finally hits noon, Nina gives us what she calls a "directed" writing assignment, where we're supposed to write without thinking too hard or editing, similar to what we did yesterday, but about a specific topic.

We're supposed to write about garbage. Literally *garbage*, as in trash, refuse, stuff you throw away. No one complains, though. After what happened with Caleb, I don't think anyone wants to be the focus of Nina's attention.

"I expect to see this at the beginning of class tomorrow," she says. "So find a spot where you can write without any intrusion and get to it."

I hustle so I can get out the door ahead of Caleb. I don't want to have to face him. I don't want him to have to face me.

And I definitely don't want anyone to guess that I'm the girl he wrote about.

I have lunch with Kelly — where she speaks nonstop about how incredible her professor is even though he's tough, and about how her high school teachers compare — then I opt to work in our room while she takes off for the campus library.

I get about a paragraph written before my eyes drift closed. I try walking around, I open the window, I even turn on my clock radio for a while, but it doesn't help. I set the alarm for dinnertime, snooze, and then after dinner, I try writing again.

At ten P.M., I'm still stuck. I don't know if it's my surroundings or the fact that I can't stop thinking about what Caleb wrote for yesterday's assignment that's screwing with my ability to finish *this* assignment. An assignment I'd bet anything *will* be graded.

Maybe it's the stupidity of the assignment that's keeping me from doing it. Writing about garbage can't possibly teach me anything.

I slam my notebook shut and decide to try something

different. I tell Kelly I'm headed to the beach, and even though I can tell she thinks I'm either: a) crazy; or b) meeting a guy and keeping it a secret from her, I go without explaining myself. With my notebook, pen, and flashlight in my backpack, I walk until I get to the end of the path. I kick off my flip-flops as soon as I get past the rockiest area, even though with my luck I'll step on a broken shell or sharp pebble.

The feel of the sand, still warm from the day's sun, is too good on my feet for me to be cautious. When I get to the gray rock, I pause, look up and down the dark shoreline, then decide to try somewhere new. I should be fine, as long as I don't go too far. I head away from the dock, walking where the sand is wet and firm underfoot, letting the waves run over my feet.

Before long, I spot the end of a washed-up tree and start to make my way toward it. Its roots are sticking up like giant fingers, and I decide if there's a good place to sit on its trunk, that's where I'll write.

I speed up, anxious to see what it looks like up close, but as I approach, I realize there's someone already there, staring out at the ocean. I can't change direction now without being totally obvious, so I try to act like I meant to walk past the tree all along and keep going.

What the hell was I thinking, walking here alone? I should have at least brought my cell so I could call 911 if some creep — like this one — follows me.

"Wynn?"

I instantly recognize the voice — soft and not quite Southern. I pause. "Caleb?"

"Yeah."

The way he says it makes it clear it's an invitation. I make my way toward the tree, my heart pounding. Whether it's from being surprised at the sound of a voice, or because it's *his* voice, I don't want to know.

"Hope I didn't scare you," he says when I get just outside of arm's reach from him. "What are you doing out here?"

I'm close enough to see him clearly now, even though it's pretty dark out. He's in a pair of faded jeans and the white Alabama T-shirt he wore the first day, when he stopped by my room. His feet are bare, toes stuck in the sand, and his Tevas are on the tree next to him.

I hold up my notebook and flashlight. "Came to write. Haven't been able to wax poetic about garbage yet."

"Did mine in my room this afternoon. I got about five pages. After today's fiasco" — he pauses, then says — "I'm sorry about that, by the way. I was sitting on the grass, near the path, because I figured I could see the whole beach from there and I could write about people-watching, since writing about the waves or the rocks and sand seemed pretty clichéd. I ended up watching more than writing, though."

I can't help it. I laugh, even though the tranquility of the beach and the fact that he's so serious and apologetic make me feel like a dorkus maximus for being so loud. "I was people-watching, too. Until I started to doodle. I think I got a full page of doodles. I was afraid if I didn't look like I was working, Nina would pounce on me."

He shakes with laughter — genuine laughter — which makes me feel less like a Minnesota goober. "I wondered! Everyone else was writing as if she might walk up behind them at any second, shoulders all hunched up" — he demonstrates for me — "and with stressed-out looks on their faces. But not you. You looked relaxed. And you were making these big, loopy motions, so it was obvious you weren't writing. I found that so funny, that everyone in their swimsuits was so intense, yet here you were without a swimsuit and goofing off."

He buries his toes in the sand and laughs, then adds, "You were the only thing worth writing about."

"And then, only a paragraph!"

"Two, if you count what I did in class this morning," he says. "Don't sell me short."

We quiet down, but it's a comfortable quiet. Like we're both amused at the situation and now can bond over it.

"Anyway, I'm really sorry if I embarrassed you." His voice is so low I can hardly hear it over the *whoosh* of a large wave connecting with the shore.

"It's okay. I mean, you didn't embarrass me. Everyone in class was probably sitting there freaked out that Nina might go through the rest of the pile and start reading theirs aloud. I doubt anyone knew or cared who it was about." Since Bayleigh's the only person who could have known, I'm hoping this is a true statement.

"I looked over at Bayleigh after Nina finished reading," Caleb said. Apparently he'd thought the same thing I did at the time. "She wasn't even paying attention. She had a nail file out under the desk and was fixing her nails."

"Well, I guess that's a good thing. Not about the nails, but that she wasn't paying attention."

I should feel awkward talking to him about this, but I don't. He apparently doesn't feel very awkward with me, either, because he reaches out and takes my hand, pulling me down to sit next to him.

He lets go the minute my rear hits the tree trunk, but I try not to think about what it means. I don't want to know if he would have grabbed Bayleigh's (well-manicured) hand if she'd been the one to walk up on him.

"Well, it solves the big mystery, meeting you out here in the middle of the night with your flashlight," he says. "Guess I know how you got all those pages written."

"Busted." I glance sideways at him. "So why are *you* out here?"

We're sitting close enough that I feel his shoulders go up and down, rather than see his shrug. "Wanted to get out of the room, I guess. See what the beach is like at night. Want me to

214

leave you alone so you can write? I won't be offended if you tell me you need privacy."

"You were here first," I point out. "And I'm not in much of a mood to write, anyway. At least not about garbage." Or anything else. I don't know why — it's more than just the fact that he's cute and smells like coconut sunscreen — but I want to hang out with Caleb, even if we don't talk. To just *be*. Part of me is nervous, like I'm stepping too far beyond my bounds simply to satisfy my curiosity. But the other, bigger part of me — the part of me run by gut instinct — feels comfortable with him and like this is the right thing to do.

A full five minutes, maybe even ten, go by as we watch the waves roll in. We don't speak. We just let our minds drift along, listening to the sound of our own breath, the roll of the surf, the occasional rustle of the wind through the tall grass on the slight ridge behind us. I try to identify constellations as the stars become brighter and brighter in the night sky. I watch as, every few seconds, a light spins in the distance. It takes me a while to realize that it must be coming from a lighthouse. I wonder if it's on an island, or if there's a peninsula that juts out into the sea that I missed seeing before.

Caleb grabs his sandals, and it's all I can do to keep from sighing out loud. I'm not ready for this to end. I think this is more fun than I've ever had just sitting with someone.

"Let's swim," he says. This time when he grabs my hand and pulls me along, he doesn't let go.

215

# Five

"Um, I'm not wearing a suit under this," I tell him as we walk.

"No big deal. Go naked or wear your underwear."

From any other guy, this would be a total line, even coming out as casually as it does from Caleb's mouth. I'm not that naive. It's one of those situational remarks a guy pops out with to give a girl an excuse to fool around without feeling like she's being a slut.

But with Caleb, I feel okay about it.

I glance up and down the beach as we get to the wet, hard-packed sand at the water's edge. No sight or sound of human activity. Caleb lets go of my hand and pulls his T-shirt over his head in one smooth motion.

I try to remember what bra I'm wearing, decide it's decent (black fabric that's sexy, yet thick enough to obscure any nipple show-through if wet) and toss my T-shirt beside his on the sand. He already has his shorts off and is walking into the water as I shed mine.

I get in the water as fast as I can, up to my waist, while he still has his back to me. While the pale thing isn't such an issue at night, the fact is I'm with a near-stranger, that near-stranger is male, and I'm in my *underwear*.

He ducks underwater, then comes back up, spraying water off his hair. "Whew! Chilly!"

I tell him I agree. It's cooler than I expected, but I've experienced worse in Minnesota. Ditto as a clump of seaweed brushes against my side. The lakes at home are always full of grass, leaves, and other floaties. But the waves — the waves are a whole new experience, carrying me up and down as each one passes. It makes me realize how powerful the ocean is and how small I am in comparison.

"So, Wynn Michaela, huh? I like that."

I smile to myself, 'cause I like it, too. And he doesn't jump to the conclusion that Wynn is short for Winifred. "Thanks. And Caleb Wilson, right?"

"Wow, good memory. Wilson's my mom's maiden name," he says.

I tell him I think that's neat that he got both his parents' last names, but I'm glad my parents didn't do that to me. My mom's Norwegian, so her last name was Walderhaug. "Wynn Walderhaug O'Malley doesn't sound as good as Caleb Wilson Rowles," I say, and he agrees.

"So tell me," he says, moving toward me in the water, "Who are you at home? Popular? Geek? Jock? Loner?"

I think it's hysterical that he asks me this, since it's what I wondered about everyone when I was in his room for pizza. "You tell me first," I say.

"Fair enough." He's silent for a moment, thinking. Then he says, "It's hard to know. My dad's in the Army, so I move a lot. Just as I'm getting into a social group, making friends, we have to move. We've been in Fort Rucker, Alabama, for two years now, and I *think* I'm in the jock crowd, but at the fringes. So if I had to pick a social identity" — he pauses and shrugs — "I guess I'd go with observer. If that makes any sense."

"You know, it does." Explains the almost-accent and his ability to adapt to dorm life — getting people in for pizza, scrounging to find a sofa — as if he's done it a dozen times before. It's just another move for him. And maybe why he's taking Creative Writing instead of one of the other courses.

"I bet you're an observer, too," he says. "I mean, besides whatever other crowd you may hang with at home. You could jump in at anytime into whatever conversation — like when you're in the cafeteria and you sit with your roommate and all the kids from Environmental Economics, or like on the night we were all having pizza — but you don't. You watch, but you do it in a way that doesn't make it obvious. Everyone else thinks you're being just as social as they are."

I almost say, "How do you know?" because it's the automatic response to all he's said, but I don't. I can tell from his expression, right now as he's floating along with the waves, why he wrote about me. Why he was curious about me. And he knows I know too. We just *get* each other. Somewhere, underneath our visible differences, we're a lot alike.

So instead, I tell him about all the things that matter to me back in Dawson, Minnesota. He asks about Mean Raymond at the Dairy Darling and Dad's job at 3M, and I ask him about his dad being in the Army and what it was like for him and his mom when his dad got sent to Afghanistan for six months. Then he tells me about all the different places he's lived, like North Carolina, Kentucky, and even Germany. I love how he describes them all — it makes me wish I could visit them, just for a little bit, so I can see what he's seen.

As he talks, he refers to himself as an Army brat, which is an expression I've heard before but would never actually call someone. But he seems as proud of it as I am of being from Dawson, even though most of the kids who are in the program with us would probably think of it as some hick nothing town, especially after they all *oooh*ed over Martha's Vineyard. But Caleb tells me he wishes he could see Dawson, just to check it all out and see Mean Raymond with his own eyes. And, he says, to see just how big the scoops really are at the Dairy Darling.

Caleb asks me if I've thought much about where I want to go to college. He came here for the summer because a friend had done the program and liked it, but he says he's not sure his parents can really afford four years of a private college. I tell him my parents are pushing for me to go to the University of Minnesota. Resident tuition.

"I want to keep my options open, though," I tell him.

"Before I left home, I sent away for tons of info on scholar-ships. Just to see what I might be able to get."

"And here I was about to be completely heartbroken."

Really? *Heartbroken?*

"I always wondered if . . . whoa! Watch out!"

A good-sized wave comes in, lifting us off our feet and car-rying us both toward the shore. Caleb's shoulder knocks against mine in the rolling surf, and we end up on our rear ends in knee-deep water. As the wave leaves us behind, he grabs my hand under the water and asks if I'm okay. I assure him that I'm fine. In fact, it was pretty fun to lose control like that.

"We have to go back soon," he says. "It's got to be close to midnight."

"Yeah, I know." I don't want this to end though. The rhythm of the water, the conversation, any of it.

"I'd much rather stay." I barely hear him say it, but his fingers tighten around mine under the water like he's going to pull me up, so we can walk back. But then the next wave hits us, covering our chests and then continuing on, and his other hand comes up to cup my cheek.

Then he's kissing me.

It's tentative. Cautious. Like when someone gives you a dessert with a strange name like *baklava* or *tiramisu* and insists that you'll like it, but you're not so sure. Since it's des-sert, though, you give it a taste.

And after a few careful bites around the edges, you discover that it's exactly what you wanted.

And you want it all.

A minute later, he stops. His lips are smiling against mine as another wave goes past us, then recedes, leaving us sitting in the middle of a sucked-out hollow in the sand. "Guess we should go," I say.

"Yeah."

He stands and helps me up. There's sand all over my legs and the back of my panties. I do my best to brush it off as I walk up the beach, then find my shorts and step in. It doesn't feel any different than if I'd been wearing a swimsuit, and I wonder if this is how Kelly felt when she changed into her bikini with the door open.

No, I decide. It's different. Kelly's change was public, almost exhibitionist. This is private. Just us and the water and the stars.

When I get my shirt on, I realize Caleb's in his shorts and Tevas, but can't find his T-shirt.

"Forget it." He gestures toward the ocean. "Bet it got carried out. We left everything too close to the water." He helps me find my notepad and flashlight, which are miraculously dry, and we make our way back toward the path, holding hands. When we're just outside the circle of light cast by the path's overhead lights, he pulls us up short.

"You going to be able to write beautiful things about garbage?"

"I'll get up early," I assure him.

"Good. I want you to get a good grade in Nina's class. You know a lot of kids in this program end up getting scholarships when they apply?"

I didn't know that. But now that I do . . . hmmm. Not that it'll change the effort I put in — I always bust my hump in class, since Mom and Dad drilled that desire into me early — but. . . .

He leans in and gives me the sweetest kiss I could ever imagine. "Let's do this again. I mean, if it's okay with you. No pressure. It's just . . . I guess I feel like we get each other."

Oh, yeah. That *is* a tingle going up my spine. I reach up to fix a lock of wet hair that's plastered against his cheek. It's cool and soft in my fingers. "I'd like that."

He grins and kisses the palm of my hand — a totally sexy move — then we let go of each other without saying anything further. As we walk back to our rooms, our bodies are a comfortable distance apart. Not because we're embarrassed or trying to distance ourselves from each other. More like what happened on the beach is our secret. A secret we want to stay that way, to keep in our own hearts.

When I get back to the room, Kelly's snoring. I change into pajamas and sit by the window, where the outdoor security lamps cast just enough light for me to write. I fill about three pages, just for myself, about the night. About Caleb and Fort

Rucker and being an observer, and about the possibilities. About how, even if things don't go any further with Caleb than they did tonight, that it's okay. I can be myself and still be just fine.

Although I know all the way into my bones that this isn't a one-night deal. This is the start of something really, really good.

"Score one for Wynn!"

I start, then turn to look at Kelly. She's sitting up in bed, the shadows cast by the security lamps making her features look downright diabolical.

"What are you talking about?"

She rubs her hands together. "Yes! I can tell from your face. Something happened out at the beach tonight and I bet it involves a guy. You gotta tell me the whole story. Like, who was there? Someone from your class? Or is he in one of the other classes? Whoa — or was it like, one of the college-aged guys? I bet it was one of the cafeteria workers. Yeah, that's it! I saw the guy dishing out the veggies giving you the once-over. Did you notice? I bet —"

"Kelly!" The *veggie* guy?

"Okay, okay. Just give me the scoop in the morning. I promise not to interrupt, and you *know* that's a huge promise coming from me!"

I crack up, because there's no way she can keep from interrupting. "Sorry, I don't kiss and tell."

"Arrgh!" She fakes like she's going to throw her pillow at me. "Okay, *fine*. I have weeks and weeks to get the info outta you."

"We'll see." It's not going to be anytime soon. This whatever-it-is with Caleb won't be the same if I discuss it.

"Well, good for you," she says. "It's always the quiet ones you gotta watch out for, isn't that the saying?"

She gives me a smile that makes me happy all the way down to my toes. She rolls over, and within minutes she's out cold again.

I smile to myself as her breathing becomes even, and then her soft, rhythmic snoring begins. I envy people who fall asleep that fast. I never have. And I know I should be trying to sleep now, but I'm nowhere near ready.

I flip to a fresh page and write about the environmental impact of garbage — since it's easy to write about what people should do to recycle, and I've never not turned in an assignment in my life — then close the notebook.

I look out at the ocean and listen to the surf. A flash of white at the water's edge, in the direction of the tree trunk, catches my attention, but then it's gone.

I wonder if it's Caleb's shirt.

I wonder if we'll find it tomorrow night.

I wonder how I ever went all these years without realizing that the best part of summer is the night.

# ★ ABOUT THE AUTHORS ★

**Niki Burnham** is the RITA-award-winning author of several popular books for teens, including the Royally Jacked series about Valerie Winslow. Burnham frequently draws on her Army brat upbringing when writing her stories. A former attorney, she now lives in Massachusetts with a blind, 20-lb. Siamese cat who stalks her relentlessly. Her next novel, *Goddess Games*, will be out in late May 2007. You can find Niki online at www.nikiburnham.com.

Between her junior and senior years of high school in Germany, Niki came back to the United States to attend a college writing program at the University of Colorado. Her experience there provided the inspiration for "Night Swimming," in which a girl from rural Minnesota attends a summer writing program at a fictional Delaware college.

A native New Yorker, **Erin Haft** is a devotee of the leisure life. When she isn't writing, hanging out with friends, or unsuccessfully trying to hail a cab, she can be found reading poolside at her club, where she holds three (count 'em, three) Ping-Pong championship titles. Who says women should stick to tennis and Pilates? Her novels include *Pool Boys* and *A Kiss Between Friends*.

If you're wondering how Erin was inspired to write "Cabin Fever," it's simple: Growing up, she *died* to get out of the city as soon as the school year ended (too hot, too many tourists, too many cute boys away on vacation), so she begged her parents to let her go to camp in Vermont every summer. And while she doesn't have a glamorous younger sister (her glamorous sister is, in fact, older), she did draw upon personal experience and a nostalgic treasure trove of camp memories when creating this story. The names, as always, have been changed to protect the guilty.

**Sarah Mlynowski** is the author of numerous novels including *Bras & Broomsticks*, *Frogs & French Kisses*, and *Spells & Sleeping Bags*. Originally from Montreal, Sarah now lives and writes in New York City. If you want to say hello, visit her web site at www.sarahm.com.

"The idea for this story came from a trip to France. My friend was working in Nice on a summer exchange program and I went to visit. Her brother happened to be visiting at the same time. This is the 'what if' story. . . ."

**Lauren Myracle** is the author of eight novels for tweens and teens, with many more in the works. Her breakout success came with the publication of the *New York Times* best-selling *ttyl,* the first-ever novel written entirely in instant messages. She holds an MFA in Writing for Children and Young Adults from Vermont College, and her work has been described by teens as "awesome," "the best ever," and "sooo funny." She was perhaps most pleased, however, by the reader who said of her work, "I can't believe it was written by a (cough, cough) grown-up."

When asked what inspired her to write "Miss Independent," Lauren says, "The entire story came to me in a dream. Just kidding! I wish stories would flow miraculously from the universe to my fingers to my computer screen, but alas. Writing is plain old-fashioned work. But *fun* work. Writing 'Miss Independent' was especially fun, because this was the very first time (true!) that I set out with the express purpose of exploring romance. And love. And cute, cute boys with quirky smiles. I tried to capture the exhilaration of truly connecting with someone, but also the self-doubt that sometimes goes along with that (and turns you into a big blob of wimpy Jell-O). You greater mortals may never experience that Jell-O-y wimpiness, but for me it's pretty much a way of life. Nonetheless, wimpiness can be overcome, and true love does occasionally prevail. Here's to human connection!"

*Take a sneak peek at*
# IN or OUT
*the new novel by Claudia Gabel*

*Rivalries. Crushes. Betrayals.*
*It's just another day in high school.*

Nola took a deep breath as she stepped off the bus with Marnie and walked up the pathway leading toward Poughkeepsie Central. The enormous redbrick building looked very imposing. It sat on top of a steep hill, behind neatly trimmed shrubbery. On the main lawn, there was a statue of the prominent and important leader of the Native American tribe who gave the town its name, and the quote *Imagine what you'll learn tomorrow* was engraved at his perfectly proportioned feet.

But Nola couldn't even bring herself to imagine what tomorrow would have in store for her, especially because within her first fifteen minutes of high school, she suffered three brief, but very embarrassing moments:

1) She'd tripped over a crack in the pathway and almost fell on top of a hottie. She just got a split second, I'm-about-to-squash-you look at him, but she could see that he was tall, lean, and dressed in a pale yellow oxford shirt with the sleeves rolled up. Luckily, Marnie grabbed Nola by her backpack and saved her from knocking him down.

2) After that mini-fiasco, Nola started to hyperventilate, so she ran into the bathroom. The boys' bathroom, that is. Marnie came to the rescue again and yanked Nola out of there before she saw anyone unzip their pants.

3) By the time she found homeroom 105, Nola was beyond flustered. And where was Marnie Fitzpatrick? Down the hall in homeroom 104 with all the other A's through G's: i.e., nowhere near Nola.

She raced over to the bulletin board by the door, lugging her huge global studies textbook with her — when the bell had rung, she hadn't found a spot for it yet in her locker. Nola saw her name on the seating chart and tried to sprint to her desk. But as she worked her way through the crowd of students, she stepped on someone's toe. Really, really hard.

The shriek was loud and high, as if it'd come from a parakeet who'd been caught in the mouth of a pit bull. But it was a girl who'd made that noise. A stunning blonde girl who appeared to have gotten dressed with her eyes closed this morning, but somehow had managed to look utterly fabulous. Nola knew from listening to Marnie-the-Fashion-Guru that you weren't supposed to cinch a bright orange floral housedress with a huge white belt or pair it with pointy red ankle boots (unless you were a celebrity or homeless or something), yet this girl was able to pull it off — no problem.

"I need to sit down," the girl moaned. A couple of people gathered around her and guided her to a desk. The girl took off her ankle boot and began rubbing her foot.

Nola was practically in tears. "I'm sorry, I'm so, so, sorry." She must have said it more than once because the girl suddenly held up her hand and said, "Whatever!" in an extremely annoyed voice.

"Do you want me to take you to the nurse?" Nola asked, even though she had no idea where the nurse's office was. Her heart was racing so fast she thought she might faint and then they'd both have to be taken away in an ambulance.

"Maybe later, when I have some feeling back in my toes!" the girl snapped.

Nola just nodded and shrank toward the back of the room. She scrunched down in her seat and hid behind her global studies textbook. She was seconds away from breaking out in hives and she didn't want anyone to witness the horror. Marnie had seen it happen many times before and was quite handy with calamine lotion.

Nola closed her watery eyes and wished really hard that somehow her best friend would appear and make everything okay.

Then there was a tap-tap on the other side of her textbook. She ignored it.

*Tap-tap.*

Nola began reading from some random chapter in the middle of *Intro to Global Studies:* The main exports of Myanmar are timber and agricultural products.

*Tap-tap.*

*The main exports of Myanmar are timber and agricultural products.*

*TAP-TAP.*

*THE MAIN EXPORTS OF MYANMAR ARE TIMBER AND AGRICULTURAL PRODUCTS!*

*TAP-TAP-TAP!*

Nola reluctantly lowered her textbook. "What?" she asked briskly. Then she noticed that she was staring directly into the hazel eyes of a boy with an oval-shaped face and messy, light brown hair. She immediately looked away.

"Just wanted to see if you were still alive," he replied with a wink.

The last thing Nola needed right now was to go

head-to-head with a smart-ass. Besides, she didn't have the guts to do it anyway. She raised *Introduction to Global Studies* in front of her face once again.

TAP-TAP.

Nola sighed in frustration and put the book down. "Yes?"

The boy grinned. "She's still alive, too."

Nola glanced over at the girl whose toe she nearly broke and saw the guy was right — she was happily chatting with a bunch of girls as if nothing had happened.

Finally there was a reason to smile. "Thanks," Nola said, grinning back.

"No problem." The boy spun around in his seat so that he was fully facing her. "But I wouldn't rule out a lawsuit."

Nola laughed in spite of her pre-hiveishness.

He extended his hand. "I'm Matt Heatherly."

Nola blinked a few times. She was a horrible conversationalist. It was one of the many drawbacks of being shy. "Oh . . . I'm Nola . . . Nola James," she stammered while shaking his hand, ever-so-lightly.

"Nice to meet you," Matt said. Then he wiped his hand on the bottom of his plain charcoal-gray T-shirt.

Nola's paranoia immediately shifted into overdrive.

Whoa, what was that about? Are my palms really sweaty? Is there a wart on my finger? Or a booger?!

But Matt acted like nothing was wrong. "So, which middle school did you go to? You don't look familiar."

Nola was still obsessing about that suspicious hand-wipe, so she could barely remember anything. "Um . . . you know," was all she could get out.

Oh my God, I'm destined to be a social leper!

Matt looked puzzled. "Huh. Well, I went to Arlington. It was okay, for a school built on a turnpike."

Nola couldn't believe it. Even though she was totally stressed out, she started laughing again.

"Our homeroom teacher is late," Matt said, gesturing at the clock above the chalkboard. "That's a good omen. Maybe school will be canceled forever and we'll be released into the wild."

"I wouldn't count on it." Nola scowled.

"You're right." Matt's grimace reappeared. "They'd probably just let us die in here."

Suddenly the classroom door flew open and a frantic woman with a rip in her dark beige stockings dashed in. She was completely disheveled and hiccuping. Nola breathed a sigh of relief: Someone was having a worse day than she was.

"I know, I know!" Loud hiccup. "I'm late!" The woman slammed her oversized, weather-beaten black satchel onto the top of her desk. "Get (hiccup) used to it."

Matt mouthed the words, "Oh boy," to Nola and turned back around in his seat very slowly. Nola swallowed hard. She didn't have to be a psychic to foresee that this teacher was going to be nothing but trouble.

"My name is Miss Lucas," the woman said as she rummaged through her bag and pulled out a folder stuffed with pieces of paper. After she'd rifled through it with great eagerness, she slammed it down on the desk as well. "We're skipping roll call today, people." Big scowl. "Can't (hiccup) find those stupid attendance sheets (hiccup) anywhere!"

Nola glanced at the clock. It was only 8:15 a.m. There was a whole day ahead of her and so far everything had gone wrong. But at least she'd met a nice boy.

That was always a good thing, wasn't it?